There was a reward of five thousand dollars for the man who could bring Barbara Davis out of Apacheria alive. Every outlaw, gunman, and scalphunter in the south-west had drifted in to Tucson, then out into Apache country, lured by the dream of easy gold. The Apaches killed some of them slowly and horribly; but still they came. Governor Bleke knew unless the girl was brought out soon, he would have a full scale Indian war on his hands. He sent for the one man who might be able to do it. A tall, slow-drawling man who wore his sixguns tied low and looked as if he knew how to use them. A Texas outlaw on the run: SUDDEN!

Other SUDDEN Westerns by Oliver Strange

SUDDEN
SUDDEN – THE MARSHAL OF LAWLESS
SUDDEN OUTLAWED
SUDDEN PLAYS A HAND
SUDDEN MAKES WAR
SUDDEN RIDES AGAIN
SUDDEN TAKES THE TRAIL
THE RANGE ROBBERS
LAW O' THE LARIAT

by Frederick H. Christian

SUDDEN AT BAY
SUDDEN – TROUBLESHOOTER
SUDDEN STRIKES BACK

and published by Corgi Books

Frederick H. Christian

Sudden Apache Fighter

CORGI BOOKS
A DIVISION OF TRANSWORLD PUBLISHERS LTD

SUDDEN—APACHE FIGHTER

A CORGI BOOK 0 552 11800 1

First publication in Great Britain

PRINTING HISTORY
Corgi edition published 1969
Corgi edition reprinted 1969
Corgi edition reissued 1971
Corgi edition reprinted 1972
Corgi edition reprinted 1974
Corgi edition reprinted 1977
Corgi edition reissued 1981

This book is set in 10pt Intertype Baskerville

Corgi Books are published by Transworld Publishers Ltd.,
Century House, 61–63 Uxbridge Road,
Ealing, London W5 5SA.
Made and printed in Great Britain by
Hunt Barnard Printing Ltd., Aylesbury, Bucks.

For H. and about time, too

CHAPTER ONE

Apaches!

They came out of the arroyo where they had lain silent throughout the desert night, the faint grey light of dawn revealing them: swift-moving, crouching figures moving with deadly purpose across the deserted ranch yard, to catch the sleeping house unawares. The cook, bustling about his early-morning chores behind the kitchen saw them, and screamed just once before he fell, gutted by the swift sweep of a razor-sharp knife.

The Chiricahuas were everywhere, running flat out now across the open space before the house, their thin screams harsh and unearthly in the chill dawn, echoing from the thick adobe walls.

Old Larrabee, the stove-up horse wrangler, had been up early. Seeing them as he ambled down towards the corral, hearing them coming, he grabbed his Winchester and ran to meet them, pumping slugs into the breech and firing as he ran, yelling at the top of his voice for help from the hands in the bunkhouse. His first shot cartwheeled one of the Apaches off his feet, his second smashed another sideways in the dirt; the third shot caught one in the thigh, slewing him around screeching in agony; and then they were on Larrabee. The long knives rose and fell and the dust fogged high over the heaving piles of bodies as the other warriors ran around it without breaking their stride.

The five riders in the bunkhouse had awakened to the sound of shouting and the explosion of shots. They spilled out of bed with their guns in their hands; there was only one explanation for such noises. They came piling out of the bunkhouse door into a murderous rain of bullets from the waiting Indians. Two of the riders wilted downwards as Jackson, the foreman, yelled hoarsely for his men to get back. Through the swirling gunsmoke he saw the lithe dark figures moving like wraiths, and emptied his sixgun at them as he rolled sidewards. Behind him, Tanner and Taylor cursed as they slid to a prone position in the dirt and laid a slicing barrage across the yard as they edged back for the shelter of the bunkhouse. Jackson frantically reloaded his revolver as his men blasted one of the Chiricahuas off the porch, but now another and another were there. Facing them defiantly stood the old, half-blind Mexican woman who had been a nurse to the family for nearly twenty years. She held her arms wide as though barring the Indians access to the door. One of them struck her aside brutally with the butt of his rifle and rushed wildly in, only to be hurled back like some broken puppet as the Navy Colt in the hands of Sarah Davis boomed not two feet from his chest. The two warriors behind him leaped back swiftly, flattening themselves against the rough mud surface of the three-foot thick adobe walls. The woman inside retreated slowly from the gaping doorway, her eyes wide, the gun in her small hands trembling slightly. Reaching the door of the bedroom, she bolted inside and slammed the door, barring it. Then, with the aid of her eighteen-year-old daughter Barbara, she pushed a heavy dressing table against it. Sarah Davis took her daughter's hand and patted it, but the ears of both the women were attuned to the sounds in the yard outside.

The three riders in the bunkhouse had managed to regain its shelter and, manning a window each, were searching the open space with their accurate rifle fire, picking off one of the warriors near the door, then the other; pinning the war party down.

Off to the right, the leader of the raiding party, an imposing figure with a jagged lightning emblem painted on his copper chest, gave a signal to one of his warriors. The squat Apache dismounted and quickly made a small fire. The others unslung the short Apache bows from their ponies, and tied dry grass around the arrowheads. When they were ready the leader nodded again, and a moment later a rain of flaming arrows arced across the brightening sky, streaking down into the tar-paper roof of the bunkhouse. The thin yellow flames licked the flimsy material, as if tasting it. Then they bit deeper, leaping as if in joy, spreading and dancing. Heavy black smoke rose high in the still morning air; within ten minutes the bunkhouse was an inferno. The three men inside wrapped blankets about their faces to shield them from the flames and made a desperate try for the ranch house. The Chiricahuas cut them down with the feral joy of hunting wolves.

Now the leader gave another signal. The warriors gathered for a moment, then hurled themselves at the house once more. They came into it panting, their musky stink filling the pretty room. In an orgy of blind destruction, the Apaches smashed the windows, ripped down the flowered curtains, splintered the furniture. One of them found a cupboard filled with bottles; they drained the whisky like water. And then they broke down the bedroom door. Sarah Davis killed two of them before they reached her.

CHAPTER TWO

'I DON'T care if it means killin' off every damn' Apache buck in the territory, Bleke – I want my girl back!' The speaker was a small, compactly-built man of about forty-five. His aggressive stance, and small shrewd eyes gave some hint of the burning drive which had made John Davis the biggest rancher in southwestern Arizona. He had come West the year after the end of the Civil War, driving before him two mules and a milk cow. Defying the elements, the warring Apaches, and the treacherous land itself, he had carved an empire out of the desert. In one terrible night, all he had worked for over the years had been reduced to ashes. Davis had returned to his ranch after a business trip to Phoenix which had necessitated him staying overnight, something he rarely did these days, to ride back with the rest of his riders. They had found the ranch a smouldering ruin, the bloated bodies of the dead strewn like tattered dolls in front of it, savagely mutilated. What he had found inside the house had overnight turned Davis's hair to grey.

Now he thrust his heavy chin forward and glowered from beneath bushy brows at the quiet man who sat listening to his tirade.

'John,' the man said. 'I know how you feel. I'm doing everything within my power as Governor—'

'Hell an' damnation! Bleke, it ain't enough!' Davis would not be silenced. 'I'm goin' to play it my way whether yu like it or not!'

'Don't you think you've caused trouble enough already, John?' Governor Bleke was a quietly-spoken man. Short, as sturdily built as his visitor, there was little about the man in his grey business suit which would have singled him out in a crowd – except perhaps the cold grey eyes. Any man who looked into them for more than a moment could scarcely fail to divine the shrewd brain, the unquestioned courage, and the determination which had made Bleke's name hated and feared by every lawbreaker in the territory, just as it was held in high esteem by the law-abiding.

'Listen to me, John,' Bleke continued. 'Ever since you posted that five thousand-dollar reward every outlaw, gunman and scalphunter in the south-west has drifted into Tucson. And then drifted out again. Out into Apache country, they've gone, to kill peaceful Indians in cold blood. They've tortured women and children, they're spilling more blood than that madman Chivington did at Sand Creek – all in the name of finding your daughter. What started as a raid by one renegade war party is building into an all-out Indian war, John, and I'm telling you – it's got to be stopped!'

'Then find my daughter!' yelled Davis. 'Yu think I want her married off to some Apache buck?'

'No, of course not, but—'

'But nothin'! Barbara was stole two months back, Bleke. Yo're no nearer findin' her now than yu was then!'

'The Army—' Bleke began.

'Don't tell me about the U.S. Cavalry, Bleke, I don't want to know. That shavetail idjut at Fort Cochise ain't got the sense to know when he's bin hit with a rock.'

'The Army patrols have been out,' Bleke persisted. 'They all hear the same thing wherever they go. The friendly Indians say that this renegade Chiricahua called Juano has your daughter.'

'On'y nobody can find 'im, right?' sneered Davis. 'So that's a mighty big help. Hell, if I knowed where he was, I'd give all my riders shotguns an' do a little Injun huntin' my own self, mebbe.'

'John, you're talking wild. I know you are worr—'

'Bleke, why don't yu tell the Army to ride into the Dragoons an' stay there until they find her?'

'I'm afraid the United States Army is not responsible to me. John, I telegraphed Washington – you were here when I did it.'

'An' they said the job o' the so'jer boys is to contain an' control, avoidin' direct clashes wherever possible. What kind of Army we got these days, anyway? They oughta be out scourin' them mountains for my girl, dammit!'

'John, you know as well as I do that there are a million places in the Dragoons where this Juano could be hiding. A regiment of cavalry couldn't find him if he didn't want to be found!'

Davis shook his head like a taunted bull. 'Shore, I know it,' he admitted. 'I just can't stand doin' nothin', that's all.' Bleke was silent for a moment. He placed his fingers in a steeple, touching his lips with his fingertips, deep in thought.

'There's probably only one man alive who could go into Apacheria and get your daughter out,' he finally announced to the rancher. 'I have sent for him.'

'One man?' exploded Davis. 'Yu must be goin' loco in yore old age, Bleke. I don't care who he is, one man ain't goin' to stand no chance at all in them mountains. I'm tellin' yu Bleke, yu got to send the Army in!'

'You aren't *telling* me anything, John,' Bleke did not raise his voice but there was a coldness in it which stilled the rancher's angry outburst. In a quieter tone, Davis asked:

'Who is this *hombre* you're so shore can do the trick?'

'His name is Green. He is a – friend of mine.'

'Green. Can't say I know the name,' Davis mused. 'Where's he from?'

'Texas,' Bleke replied.

'What is he?' snorted Davis. 'Some kind o' half-breed?'

'No,' Bleke said. 'He's white – in every sense of the word. I believe he spent some years as a boy among the Piutes.'

'Yu seem to set a lot o' store by him.'

'He hasn't let me down yet,' was the quiet reply.

Davis hesitated for a moment, then shrugged. 'Bleke, if yu say so, I believe yu. I don't reckon one man can last ten minutes from the time the 'paches spot him, but . . .' He thrust out his hand, and the Governor shook it; the two regarded each other with mutual respect. Bleke did not particularly like Davis, but he respected the man's drive, and his achievements. Without such men, this vast land, so full of riches and wealth, a whole new empire which would one day take its proud place on the roll of the United States, would still be an empty desert.

'I'll do the very best I can, John,' Bleke promised. 'I know I can speak for Green, too. Now – will you withdraw your reward offer?'

Davis shook his head. 'It ain't that I don't trust you, Bleke, although I'm guessin' yu set a mite too much store by this Green jasper. It's just that as long as the reward stands, there's men out there lookin' for my gal, an' one o' them might just find her. Tell yore man he'll be welcome to the gold if he pulls it off. But so will any other man who brings her in – an' I don't care if he's the biggest cut-throat who ever wore boots. I'm right sorry, Bleke, but them's my feelin's.'

'I'm sorry too,' Bleke answered, regret in his voice. 'It's going to make my man's job that much more difficult. The Apaches need little enough excuse to kill now. With your cut-throats at their foul work, they will need even less.'

'If he's as good as yu seem to think he is, he'll make it,' Davis said unfeelingly, picking up his hat. 'Yu tell him he'll be well paid for the risks he's takin'.'

'He isn't doing it for the money,' Bleke reminded Davis coldly.

'That's what they all say until they see the dollars,' Davis barked. 'Never met a man yet couldn't be bought. Some cost a mite more, that's all.'

'You couldn't buy this one,' Bleke told him, softly.

'I'll wait an' see,' Davis said, and marched out of the office, banging the door behind him. Bleke shook his head. Power and money had not absolutely corrupted Davis, but they had certainly made him accustomed to having things his own way. Frustration made a man like that strike out blindly, and fall back upon the belief that money could buy anything. Bleke crossed his office to the window and looked out upon the scene below. Tucson was a busy little town, still retaining many evidences of its Spanish origins. To the north, gleaming white in the sun, lay the old Mission San Xavier del Bac, founded by the *padres* three hundred years before. Below him stretched the bustling street, with its houses of sunbaked adobe, wide patios and long shaded porches. On the crowded sidewalks rough-clad miners from the copper mines at Santa Rita jostled with local men in dark business suits. Bleke picked out slow-moving Mexicans clad in trousers tight at the waist and flared out at the ankle, a flash of gaudy sash at the waist, the swart faces shaded by embroidered sombreros; the dusky-eyed senoritas who sent shy glances from the folds of their mantillas at passing cowboys; and on all sides, the mixture of tongues: American and Spanish. Somewhere a guitar was being strummed. The air was soft, the hard sky blue. Far to the north, two days' ride away, rose the mountains, and in them lay the strongholds of the Apache. They were massing up there, Bleke knew, and they were talking war, a big war to sweep the hated white man out of their country for all time. Bounty hunters stoked the fires of hatred with every warrior they ambushed. It was an evil business, an evil trade encouraged by the Mexican Government, which had put a price of fifty pesos on the scalp of an Apache warrior, twenty five for a woman, and ten for a child. Bleke shook his head; he was powerless to stop it. The added incentive of Davis's reward had sent the scum of the south-west into Apacheria. The Apaches had killed many of them, slowly and horribly; but still more came to kill innocent men, women and children – for in Mexico no questions were asked as to the tribe of Apaches, whether warlike or peaceful, that the scalp had been taken from – and to rouse even the non-violent tribes into retaliation. Finally, the whole Apache nation would be fired into the bloodiest uprising that the south-west had ever seen. And therein lay the importance of John Davis's daughter: if she could be brought out of Apacheria alive, then the lure of the reward would be gone, and the lawless ones might move on to new pastures, leaving the territory with a chance at least of solving its problems with the Apaches. Bleke shook his head; it was a big responsibility to give to one man, even one in whom he had such faith.

A knock on the door interrupted his thoughts, and he turned to see a tall, slim man, wide shouldered and deeply tanned, coming into his office. Bleke's sombre expression changed to a warm smile.

'Jim,' he exclaimed, 'it's good to see you! Here, let me look at you!'

Still under thirty, slim of hip, standing with the loose grace of a natural athlete, Bleke's visitor wore ordinary cowboy rig. His clothes, although worn, were neat; the lean, clean-shaven face so deeply bronzed as to almost hint at Indian blood, but the high cheekbones were absent, and there were lines of good humour about the mouth and friendliness in the level, grey-blue eyes. His opening words were whimsical.

'That feller outside warn't shore he oughta let me in here, totin' these.' His hands lightly brushed the tied-down matched sixguns nestling in holsters on his thighs. Bleke's face was serious.

'You're probably going to need those, my boy,' he said. 'Sit down and let me tell you why I asked you to come.'

The man from Texas sat down and listened gravely while the Governor spoke, and went on speaking for perhaps an hour. When Bleke had finished, the puncher whistled softly. 'She's a man-sized job, seh,' he remarked with a tight grin, 'but I'll go yu.'

'I have no right to ask you, Jim,' Bleke said, slowly. The cowboy grinned. 'Shucks,' he drawled. 'If yu ain't, who has?' He stood up, ready to leave. Bleke extended his hand, and the puncher took it firmly.

'Good luck, Jim,' the Governor said.

'I'll prob'ly need some,' was the laconic reply.

CHAPTER THREE

'Reckon we've arrove, Nig,' the rider said, reining in on the crest of a bluff to survey the scene before him. As far as the eye could see the mountains marched along the horizon, slate grey and purple and black. Towards them sloped undulating hills, dotted with mesquite and the sentinel-like saguaro cactus which grows only in this part of the southwest. The sun in the brazen sky was a blinding ball of molten light, beating down relentlessly upon the empty, unprotected land. Beneath it, unseen, the myriad desert creatures led their lives. There a lizard scuttled across a sunlit space to the cool refuge of darkness beneath a huge rock. The landscape was harsh and grey, and a dust as fine as face powder floated gauzily upwards with each hint of breeze that whispered among the desert plants: ocatillo, mescal, Spanish dagger.

Across the still and silent land the lone rider moved, antlike against the barren jumble of rock and sand and sky. The big black horse, its glossy pelt shining with sweat, cantered easily onwards, the pack mule following docilely behind; upwards towards the mountains, hardly visible in the wilderness, its rider slouched in the saddle, sombrero tilted forward. But there were eyes as keen as those of the mountain eagle in this land, and they saw the man, knew he was alien; and the messages moved across the land. *White man coming. Alone.* No man crossed Apacheria whom the Apache did not see.

Green eased his seat in the saddle and wiped the dust and sweat out of his eyes. 'Reckon I know what a boiled aig feels like now,' he muttered aloud, pulling the horse to a stop. Dismounting, he made a small fire, piling branches from a creosote bush upon it and laying a blanket loosely over the smoking pile. After a moment he swept the blanket aside, and a balloon of grey smoke soared up. Twice Green repeated this procedure, and then kicking sand over the fire to extinguish it, he remounted and pushed his horse forward once again.

'I'm shore hopin' that smoke makes 'em curious,' he told his horse. 'I'm guessin' folks crossin' this country don't usually announce their presence.'

The stallion snorted as if in reply, and cantered on. They were moving now into a long, rocky defile and on both sides the beetling walls rose stark towards the burning sky. The chuckling sound of a wild turkey came from the shadowed gorge ahead, and the stallion's ears flicked forward. 'Easy, Nig,' Green told his mount. Guiding the animal with his knees, he ostentatiously lifted his hands so that the absence of his gunbelt could be clearly seen.

'Mighty early in the day for a turkey to be gobblin',' he said aloud. 'Wouldn't mind bettin' he's got mighty funny-lookin' feathers.'

Keeping his hands up high, Green urged the black on into the defile. Nigger stepped cautiously, edgily; the pack mule dragged a little on its lead rope.

Again the turkey gobbled, and this time an answering call came from higher up the canyon wall. Green sat tense in the saddle, his keen eyes flickering across the faceless stone cliffs. No movement caught his eye, no tiny stone slide or dust puff betrayed the presence of anyone but himself in the canyon.

'They're shore there, all the same,' he said to himself. 'I'm playin' in luck so far: they ain't gunned me down. Mebbe I've got 'em curious.' Eyes moving alertly, ready for the first sign of a hostile move, he headed on up the canyon. Further along, the floor of the defile opened into a wide, oval-shaped clearing with a brackish pool of water formed by seepage from the rocks at one side. Green kneed his animals over to it, and swung down from the saddle. He began unhurriedly to unfasten the pack on the mule's back, swinging it down to the ground and unrolling it in one sweeping gesture. On the blanket lay trade goods: beads, mirrors, some knives, and one thing more: a slim, graceful, deadly-looking Winchester carbine, the sun picking a dull shine from its barrel even in this gloomy place. Green stood by the spread blanket, his eyes scanning the edge of the rim above him. Nothing moved.

Then without warning there was a warrior on a ledge not thirty feet above his head, an old Springfield rifle trained unwaveringly upon the man below. The Apache yelled something and his voice echoed from the enclosing canyon walls, causing the horses to toss their heads and move nervously. 'Easy, there,' Sudden told the animals, 'Easy now. He's just callin' his sidekicks.' His soft tone quietened the animals and he turned, moving very slowly, and showed both his hands held high and well away from the body to the Apache on the ledge.

Unarmed the movement said. He made another sign. *Come, see.* The right hand touched the heart and then opened out palm forward. *Friend.* And a sign again: *Come, see.*

The Apache on the ledge made the shrill, high, shouting noise again, and it was echoed in a different tone and then Green saw them all. They rose from the earth as if some sorcerer had conjured them from the very dust. Their oiled bodies were grey where they had rolled in the dirt to camouflage themselves, rendering them practically invisible until they moved. Eight of them, he counted silently, all armed with bows, arrows half-pulled, ready to be released instantly at the slightest sign of hostility. The black paint on their faces showed that they were a war-party. Green made the sign of friendship again. Knowing that many Apaches understood Spanish, he called out to them. '*Estoy amigo!*' he shouted. '*Tengo cosas finas. Mira!*'

The Apache on the ledge motioned with the rifle. His gesture was as plain as a spoken command: *stand away!* Green shrugged. He had told them he was a friend, that he had fine things. Come and look, he had invited them. Now it was in the lap of the gods; all he could do was hope that they would be intrigued, come down and talk. They could just as easily kill him and take them anyway; he was gambling on their wondering why he would have come so deep into their stronghold, announcing himself on the way, with so little to trade.

'If they ain't,' he told himself. 'I'll be shakin' hands with Saint Peter any minnit.' Or Old Nick, he added silently.

The Apache on the ledge was arguing with the others; Green could hear the angry, guttural sounds. You didn't need to be Apache to know an argument when you heard one. The man on the ledge seemed to be the leader of the war-party. He was heavily-built, but tall, albeit with the barrel chest typical of the race. A greasy red rag held the long, loose hair out of the Apache's eyes, which gleamed like coals above the high, prominent cheekbones. Finally, the man made an impatient gesture and then led the way down the side of the hill. He moved in long, easy, loping strides, as graceful as a mountain lion.

'An' about as friendly,' Green murmured.

The other warriors followed, bringing in their wake a small slide of stones and dust. They came warily forward, ready for any movement, their bows fully drawn and the deadly arrows trained upon the white man. Green stood as still as stone. The sharp animal smell of the Apaches assailed his nostrils as they clustered around him, and then fell jabbering upon the goods lying on the blanket, passing the Winchester from hand to hand, cocking and uncocking the weapon. Only the leader stood aloof, his deep dark eyes fixed like a snake upon the white man.

'Why have you come into our land?' he asked suddenly in English. 'What you want here?'

'To trade,' Green told him.

'Worthless trash!' the Apache snapped. 'White man does not come into stronghold to make trade with trash. Why you make smoke first to tell you come?'

'I didn't want to get killed afore I talked trade with yore people,' Green replied.

'Trade!' the Apache scoffed. 'Nothing worth trading except gun. Manolito take gun and kill you anyway.'

'I got some other things,' Green told him.

'Where?' snarled the Apache. 'I not see. You got nothing. Maybe you scalphunter, think to find one, two Apache and kill them for scalp.'

'I'm no scalphunter,' Green told him levelly. 'I come to trade. I got no guns; how could I kill any o' yore people?'

'Maybe with trick,' the Indian said, but Green saw that the biggest risk of all had paid off. He had no guns, and this impressed the Apache, who now said: 'What you want trade for? Yellow metal for which white-eyes fight like coyotes?'

Green shook his head. 'Not gold. I'm lookin' for a white girl stolen by yore people.'

Manolito's eyes flashed for a moment with cunning, and then he laughed harshly. 'You will not find her,' he gloated. 'She is far from here.'

'How far?'

'Many suns travel,' the Apache replied, but Green knew somehow that the man was lying. The girl was somewhere in this stronghold, perhaps very near; she might even be in the camp from which this party had come. Green shrugged. 'That's too bad,' he said. 'I could've made a good trade for her.'

'You have nothing to trade but your life,' grated the Apache, 'and we take that anyway.'

'Be a pity,' shrugged the cowboy. Something about his

very air puzzled the Apache. The heavy brows knitted, and again Manolito made an impatient gesture. Green knew his only chance was to keep the Apache puzzled; the moment the initiative passed out of his hands, the Indians would kill him as thoughtlessly as if he were an insect.

'Take me to where the girl is,' he demanded. 'Then you'll find out what I got to trade.'

One of the warriors spoke impatiently in Spanish. 'Kill him and let us go from here.'

'Take me to the girl,' insisted Green. 'What yu scared of?' The Apache drew himself upright, fierce pride on his face.

'Manolito fears no man!' he screeched.

'So he says,' sneered Green. 'Go ahead, then, kill me. What kind of bravery is that – the bravery of squaws? Does Manolito do women's work?'

The Apache stared at him. This slow-speaking white man was like no other he had ever encountered. There was no sign of fear, none of the begging, abject terror which Apaches aroused in the pitiful white captives they took. Green watched their faces. The other warriors, their craggy visages alight with curiosity, were intrigued by the exchange, and clustered around their leader and the white man.

'You speak brave,' Manolito said eventually. 'Do you die as bravely?'

'I'll make yu a fair offer,' Green said. 'Give me a chance to fight for my life.'

Again the Indian frowned. Green smiled to himself; the gambit might just work, although it was fraught with the most deadly peril to himself.

'Still, that's the name o' the game,' he mused to himself.

'You wish to fight with Manolito?' the Apache frowned.

Green nodded grimly. 'For a bargain.'

'What bargain is this?'

'Yu kill me, that's the end of it,' Green said. 'How about if yu don't?'

'It is unlikely.'

'But if yu don't?' Green persisted. 'Will yu take me to the place where the girl is?'

The warrior who had spoken before made an impatient sound. 'Kill him and be done,' he grumbled. Manolito held up a hand. 'Wait!' he snapped. 'Maybe this white-eye will give us sport. We will see if he fights as well as he boasts!' He held up a wicked-looking knife. 'With the knife?' he said. It was a question, and Green nodded his confirmation. 'Is it a bargain?' he asked.

Manolito's face went dark, and cunning touched the flat eyes. 'We will talk of it – afterwards.' There was a cold and eager smile upon his thin lips.

'The promise of Manolito is good enough for me,' Green said, gravely. 'I know he will honour it.'

'Manolito will not need to honour it,' the Apache snarled. He turned and uttered a sharp command. The other warriors moved back from the two men, squatting down on the rocks, their faces impassive but their eyes alight with interest. Fighting with the knife was a skill held in high esteem by the Apaches, and they were interested to see how the white man would fare against their leader. They had seen Manolito fight, and were in no doubt about the outcome of this affray, but they would watch him toy with this pale-skinned madman, and destroy him slowly. It would be a good story to tell around the fires tonight; they would tell the women and the young boys how the Americano who had challenged the leader of the Fox Lodge of the Chiricahuas had been taunted, teased, reduced to shambling helplessness as Manolito had taken away from him first the use of his right hand, then his right leg, and then his left hand, his left leg, and finally . . .

Manolito made a sign and one of the warriors tossed him a knife, the twin of the one Manolito had earlier brandished. It was a Bowie knife, with a blade nearly eight inches long, razor-honed and glinting wickedly in the sunlight. Souvenirs from some raid into Texas or Mexico, no doubt; the thought of the settlers killed to obtain these weapons lit a fire of cold wrath in Green which flamed beneath his cool exterior. These were raiding Apaches. They fell like the wrath of Satan upon defenceless ranches, killing like senseless animals. Bleke had described the slaughter at the Davis spread; maybe some of these warriors had been there. The thought hardened Green's resolve, and his lips tightened into a thin line.

Manolito stuck the two knives into the ground, side by side, with only the hafts protruding upwards. Then he paced six steps from them and drew a line in the dust with his heel. He repeated the procedure on the opposite side and motioned Green to the mark he had made for him. 'Do you understand what must be done?' he asked harshly.

'I know the Apache way,' was the quiet reply. Green readied himself even as Manolito took his position and turned crouching, poised for the first fast dangerous diving snatch for the knives. Green knew how the Apaches fought; Manolito would move hard and fast. He recalled the way that the Apache had come down the side of the arroyo, poised, flawless, as arrogant as a young stag. Manolito's move would come without a hint of warning; he must be ready for it. The Indian's eyes never left those of his opponent. The two men circled warily, never moving forward from the perimeter of the invisible circle, edging crabwise around the centre-point marked by the two knife hafts. Manolito swooped like a hawk for the knives and his hand was on the haft of one in a fraction of a second, his left foot sweeping across to kick the other knife out of the ground away from his opponent's grasp. But Green had allowed the Apache that moment's start, relying upon his own superb reflexes; even as Manolito's hand closed upon the knife-haft, Green's left hand was clubbing downwards. It caught the Apache as he bent, his left foot still moving, truly off balance, smashing Manolito face down in the dust as Green, his hold firm and sure upon the haft of the second knife, sprang lithely backwards and flicked the knife blade upwards and across as Manolito rolled desperately clear. A gasp escaped the watching Apaches as the two men parted. The white man had drawn first blood! Across the Apache's chest ran a knife-thin dark line which slowly thickened and oozed red. A frown darkened Manolito's haughty face, and then he tossed his head proudly, edging once more around the perimeter of the undrawn circle. The haft of the knife lay in his palm, his thumb lying loosely along it, controlling the movement of the blade, weaving it in and out. The glittering blade flickered and dipped and constantly shifted; Green's, held in identical fashion, moved with no less liquid fluidity. Parrying, testing, probing the other's defence, the two men awaited an opening, their breath rasping in the silence. A slashing stroke on the part of Green; a quick leap back by the Apache, then a counter thrust, parried. Then back to the weaving, watchful circle. Both men held their left hands high, fingers loosely spread. If the other came in, this hand would clamp down upon the opponent's knife wrist and then a test of sheer brute strength would ensue. Again Manolito lunged forward without warning, wheeling in mid-jump on his right foot, slashing wickedly across Green's guard and then back again, his razor-keen blade slicing through the material of the Texan's shirt, drawing a slim finger of pain across the tensed muscles of his left arm. Green felt a cold chill; Manolito had tried to render his left arm useless and had missed by only a hair's breadth.

Again the Apache lunged, and again Green parried. His eyes narrowed. Manolito was trying to cut him down slowly rather than going for a quick kill. The fact gave Green an edge, a superiority which he could use to his own advantage. He circled, waiting for the lunge he knew would come again. Once more the Apache came whipping in, but this time instead of springing back from the thrusting blade, Green swerved like an eel, twisting his body so that the murderous blade slid harmlessly under his left arm. Green immediately clamped his arm rigidly against his side, trapping Manolito for a brief moment in his grinding grip. In that same brief moment, he stamped down with all his strength upon the Apache's bare foot. The high heel of his boot ground into the Indian's instep and Manolito tore himself away, howling with anguish, his face contorted with hatred and pain.

'Now you die, white-eye!' he screamed. 'Now you die *quick!*' He came in low and hard, the knife point moving in a short vicious arc designed to disembowel the white man. Green saw the move coming; he had deliberately enraged the Indian to make him once abandon caution. He parried Manolito's thrust with his own blade, which shivered into spanging fragments from the jarring contact. In that half second of contact, Green was moving. His left arm went around the Indian's neck, his left leg firmly behind the Apache's left thigh. A bending, sweeping, half-turn and Manolito went up and over in a flailing welter of arms and legs, the wicked Bowie knife bouncing from his hand as he hit the baked earth with a bonebreaking thud. Green had followed through, moving forward, diving to scoop up the fallen weapon and to pin the stunned Manolito to the ground, Green's left forearm across the Apache's throat, the right pressing the gleaming blade flat against Manolito's jugular vein. The watching warriors had started to their feet, weapons ready. Green pulled Manolito's head back viciously, his fist bunched in the greasy hair.

'Will yu live or die?' he gritted. 'Speak!'

Manolito's black eyes blazed with impotent rage, and he heaved his body in an attempt to loosen the iron grip, but to no avail. Green saw the decision form in the Apache's eyes; Manolito spat out the words: 'Manolito yields.' Green tossed the knife aside and stood upright, allowing the Indian to rise to his feet. He ignored the weapons pointed at him and the threatening sounds the warriors made: they would not kill unless Manolito told them to. These next ten seconds were fraught with more danger than any which had passed: how would Manolito take his defeat? Green made a big show of slapping the dust from his clothes and not looking at Manolito, allowing time for the Apache to assimilate and adjust to what had happened. He looked up at a touch on his shoulder to see the Apache regarding him with a strange look in his eyes, something as akin to admiration as any Apache could feel for one of the alien race he had been taught all his life to hate.

'Is it in your thoughts that I will let you live?' Manolito asked harshly.

'Manolito is an Apache,' Green said gravely. 'This is Manolito's country. I remind him only of his promise.'

'You still wish to see the girl? Even if perhaps you will die anyway?'

Green nodded. 'That's what I come for.'

Manolito shook his head, then again he reached out and touched the Texan's shoulder.

'You are a brave man. Let there be a truce between us and we will see what will be.' He turned to his warriors, and uttered a sharp command in guttural Apache. The blanket and the trade goods were quickly rolled up and lashed to the back of the packmule. Manolito gestured for Green to mount his horse; the Apache thrust the Winchester into a loop on his own saddle. Green watched as the Apaches mounted their wiry little mustangs, milling into a compact group, awaiting the word from their leader.

'You come with,' Manolito said, pointing at Green. Then to his warriors, he yelled '*Vamonos!*' and they thundered in a tight-knit cavalcade up along the arroyo and deeper into the silent heart of Apacheria.

CHAPTER FOUR

THEY rode up a straight narrow gully bare of vegetation, and then the gully turned sharply right and upwards, and they were in the camp of the Apaches and the Indians were all around them. There was no noise, no shouting, only the yapping of half a dozen mangy dogs which frolicked around the hoofs of the horses. The black obsidian Apache eyes watched as Manolito led the party into the camp, which lay scattered across the top of a mesa, looking down over the edge of the cliff upon the country below.

'Mighty well chosen spot,' was Green's unspoken thought. 'Take a small army to get anywhere near this place.' He looked unflinchingly into the eyes of the warriors surrounding him as he dismounted, tense and ready for any overt move. Nobody laid a hand upon him, however. Their faces were sullen and impassive; their glances flicked towards Manolito for their cue. Green realized now that his captor was a leader among these people; Manolito's prisoner would not be harmed without his authority. A boy stepped forward to take the reins of Green's horse. Green stopped him with a gesture and spoke to the Apache.

'Tell the boy not to try to ride my horse,' he said. 'Or the horse will kill him.'

Manolito looked up and for a moment there was a flash of humour in the dark eyes. He nodded, and said something in rapid Apache to the boy.

'I tell him horse be like good squaw,' Manolito said. 'Let only one man handle.' A grin touched the dark visage, and then vanished as the Apache gestured Green to follow him. Manolito led the way to a wickiup on the far side of the cleared space in the centre of the camp. Outside it he motioned the Texan to stop, and gave a command to a squaw standing nearby. She went into the wickiup and came out after a moment with a young girl, dragging the reluctant captive none too gently. The girl made no resistance but simply stood there, eyes downcast, blinking in the sunlight. Then her eyes rose, and seeing Green, filled with bright hope which fled as she saw the absence of weapons and realized that he, too, was a prisoner.

'Take it easy, ma'am,' Green told her. 'Don't say nothin'.' She looked at him, stifling her surprise at the confident tone, her eyes moving from him to Manolito and back again. The Apache asked a question: 'Is this the woman you seek?' 'I don't know,' Green said honestly. 'Let me speak with her.'

Manolito nodded his permission and Green stepped forward, taking a closer look at the girl. She was dressed in Apache clothes: white buckskin skirt and blouse loosely fitting her slight frame, and tattered old moccasins. Her hair was matted and dirty, but it was blonde; and the eyes were a clear pale blue in the sunburned face.

'Is yore name Barbara Davis?' Green asked her. She nodded.

'Have – have you come to take me – home?' she whispered.

'That's the general idea,' he said with a grin which he hoped would encourage her. 'But we ain't out o' the woods by a long stick. Have these warwhoops – hurt yu?'

She shook her head. 'A warrior named Juano owns me,' she said in a low voice. 'I am being saved for . . . marriage.'

'Easy, now,' he told her. 'Let's see what we can do.' Again the girl nodded. She looked cowed and frightened and very tired; none of this surprised the puncher, who well knew that Apache prisoners were cruelly worked, and the women treated them sometimes dreadfully. But they had not broken the girl's spirit; perhaps there was yet a chance that he could get her out of here. He faced Manolito again.

'This is the one,' he said. Manolito nodded.

'So.' He put no emphasis on the word. 'She does not belong to me. You will speak with another.'

He turned and gave an order to one of the nearby braves who pushed his way through the throng. After a moment or two, there was a small commotion at the rear of the crowd of watching Apaches and a scowling warrior pushed his way forward. He was young, less than thirty, and moved with an arrogant grace and upright bearing which made him seem taller than his medium height. On his right arm he wore a copper band, and across his muscular chest streaked a jagged white paint line signifying lightning. This design was worked in beads upon the insteps of the high Apache boots and on the buckskin breechclout which was the man's only clothing. His high cheekbones and lizard-like eyes gave his face a cruel intensity. He stepped haughtily in front of Green, not deigning to even glance at the girl, who shrank away as he approached.

'My brother has brought you here,' he ground out. 'You will not leave this place!'

Green shrugged. 'Like I been sayin' all along: that'd be a pity. I reckoned we might do some tradin'.'

The Apache sneered. 'Juano does not trade with white-eyes.'

'Even for "the guns that fire for ever"?' asked Green.

Again Juano sneered. 'I see no guns,' he said, looking around in an exaggerated pantomime of searching which drew delighted chatters from the watching Indians. Green held up a hand. 'I do not play games like Juano,' he said flatly. 'Manolito has such a gun. I brought it for you to see.'

'It is so,' Manolito confirmed stepping forward. He thrust the carbine into Green's hands, and Green turned to face Juano.

'Take the rifle, Juano. Examine it. With ten more such rifles a man could be a great leader of his people.'

Juano grabbed the Winchester, his hands running over the smooth stock and the metal receiver. For a moment his wicked eyes touched Manolito's as if in challenge. Then, without a word, he levered the action, aimed the rifle point blank at Green, and pulled the trigger.

The click sounded loud in the sudden stillness. It was followed by a long exhalation of breath from the watchers.

'It ain't loaded, o' course,' Green said with a faint smile. Juano smiled, too, but there was lurking evil in his eyes.

'You think Juano trade girl for one empty rifle? You think Juano a fool. Juano kill you and keep gun. So!'

Again Green shrugged. 'If yu do that, then yu are a fool,' he said coldly. 'Yu'd never find out where the rest o' the rifles are.'

Dark cunning flooded Juano's eyes, and he turned to Manolito and rattled off a speech in Apache. Manolito listened and then shook his head. More vehemently, Juano spoke again, and once more Manolito refused.

'I'm guessin' he's askin' Manolito to let him torture me to find out where the guns are, an' Manolito's sayin' no,' Green told himself.

'Yu set the girl an' me free, an' I'll take yu where the rifles are,' he told Juano. The Apache paused in his harangue, thought for a moment, and then nodded. It made no difference if Manolito refused him permission to kill the white-eye now. When he led them to the guns, Juano would kill him then; the girl too. She was too thin and not strong enough to make a good wife. He would get the guns and then kill them both.

'It is agreed,' he announced haughtily. 'You will tell where guns are.'

'Yu musta misheard me,' Green told him. 'I said I'd *take* yu to 'em.'

Anger touched Juano's face. 'I think maybe we kill you now,' he said offhandedly.

'Then yu'd never get yore guns,' Green said flatly.

He watched pride fight with cupidity in the Apache's

eyes, sure of the outcome. His instinct told him that the renegade Juano was ambitious, perhaps wished to topple Manolito as leader of the tribe. With Winchesters he would be a big man; this was the basis of Green's gamble. That it was a far-fetched and desperate one he knew; but the only one that might trigger the peculiar Apache mentality.

'Speak,' Juano commanded. 'I listen.'

'I'll take yu to where the rifles are buried. When we get there, yu turn me an' the girl loose, let us ride away free. That's the deal.'

'How many guns?' Juano snapped. 'Ten,' Green replied.

'Not enough for girl,' Juano sneered.

Green shrugged. 'All I got. If it ain't enough, yu better just kill me an' be done with it.'

It took cold nerve to call Juano's bluff, but Green had a hunch that the Apache was simply testing him. A nod from Juano confirmed his guess.

'We will ride at first light,' Juano said. 'Take him away!' Juano pushed the girl back into his wickiup and strong hands grabbed Green's arms, half-dragging and half-carrying him across the clearing to another wickiup. His hands were lashed behind him with rawhide thongs, and then his feet were bound. Thus trussed, he was pushed sprawling into the wickiup, where he fell headlong upon a buffalo hide rug. It was gloomy and stuffy inside the wickiup and the ever-present Indian smell was thick, almost tangible. Outside, the Texan could hear the barking of dogs, the chattering of the squaws as they cooked the evening meal, the peaceful sounds of the village going about its normal business. Presently the odours of cooking drifted into the wickiup and Green licked his lips. He realized that he had not eaten since the morning, and that he was as hungry as a wolf.

'I reckon I'd about manage mule-meat right now,' he mused aloud. 'An' I'm bettin' if I get anythin' at all, that's what it's likely to be.'

No food was brought to him, however, and he lay in the darkness for some hours. Then the flap of the wickiup was lifted and he looked up to see Manolito standing there. The Apache regarded him without expression.

'Juano has made trade,' he said. 'The woman is Juano's. I have protected you here. I can do no more.'

'I'm grateful for Manolito's protection,' Green said gravely. 'I hope one day we may meet in peace.'

Manolito scowled. 'Your people kill my people,' he said. 'They take the hair of our women and our young children. Their spirits cannot sleep. We want only peace but it cannot be while these things happen.'

'Mebbe they can be stopped,' Green said earnestly. 'Mebbe there's a chance—'

'Tell it to Juano!' snapped Manolito. 'My people no longer heed my words when I speak peace. Soon Juano will lead Apache.' He stopped, his face limned with harsh and sorrowful lines. 'You are brave,' he said, eventually. 'Are there many like you among your people?'

Green nodded. 'We ain't all scalphunters, Manolito.'

Without answering, Manolito wheeled around and stalked out of the wickiup, leaving the Texan to frown at his retreating back. Manolito had lived up to his word; he would not allow it to be broken. But he had made it clear that once they were away from the camp, Juano would conclude his trade any way he saw fit. Green shrugged; again he prayed that his plan would not misfire. Alone, he would have faced the morrow without misgivings; but with the girl to protect, he had to play his longest hunch.

'Well, I reckon worryin' ain't goin' to change it none,' he said, wryly, and as the night slipped its shadowy mantle across the mountains he tried to sleep, well aware that tomorrow's ordeal would require every ounce of nerve he could summon.

CHAPTER FIVE

GREEN was awakened roughly in the chill of dawn by an armed warrior. A squaw carrying a plate of cooked deer meat and *tortillas* came into the wickiup. She was herself an example of the savage ruthlessness of her race. Still comparatively young, she might once have been almost a beauty, but the absence of a nose transformed her into a hideous hag. This was the Apache punishment for infidelity, the wicked disfiguration which marked a woman for the rest of her life as worthless and discarded. Day by day her punishment would go on until death released her. An object of scorn – for her mutilation was the badge of her offence – life could offer her nothing but bitterness, and yet she clung to it. She cackled derisively as she placed the food before the prisoner, who, despite himself, shrank back from the scarred face. A sharp word from the Apache at the door flap and the squaw slunk submissively away. But this reminder of the ways of the Apache was not lost upon the Texan.

'I better not give that Juano feller an inch,' was his meaningful comment to himself. With his bound hands now released, he fell upon the food with gusto, ignoring the guard. Green knew that the provision of food did not indicate any remission in the savage hatred his hosts felt for him. 'They just don't want me to keel over afore I hand them the Winchesters,' he reflected. 'Don't taste none the wuss for that though.' The meal quickly demolished, he rolled a quirly from the making's in his pocket. As he lit the cigarette the Apache grunted a command, and gestured with the rifle barrel towards the entrance of the wickiup.

'Time to go, huh?' Green asked, whimsically. 'Don't I get no cawfee?'

The Indian grunted again and made a menacing gesture with the rifle, whereupon the Texan shrugged and got to his feet. Outside, the camp was a hive of activity. The Apaches were already mounted and awaiting the appearance of their leaders. Juano came out of his wickiup; Green saw Manolito step into the daylight at the same moment that he himself emerged into the lightening dawn. Green saw the girl being helped on to a sorry-looking pony, and a grim expression settled on his face.

'They ain't takin' no chances,' he muttered to himself. 'If we try to run for it, that bag o' bones ain't goin' to get far.'

He allowed no hint of these thoughts to appear on his face, however, but mounted impassively and rode to the centre of the encampment. Juano wheeled his horse around; Green saw that there was fresh war paint on the Apache's face.

'You will lead,' Juano told him. 'If there is treachery, the girl will die first.'

A glance over his shoulder showed Green that Barbara Davis was being held back in the centre of the band. Her chin lifted bravely as she caught his eye, and he smiled. He counted fifteen warriors mounted.

'Too many to fight, an' no chance o' runnin',' he observed. 'Mebbe I'd better try thinkin' up a few good prayers.'

He touched Nigger's flanks with his unspurred heels – the stallion had never needed such goads to give of his best – and led the cavalcade forward at an easy pace down the ravine towards the open plain. Immediately before him the ground fell away in a series of wide, flat steps, dotted with the ever-present cactus and sagebrush, leading down to the deceptively flat-looking country below. Green knew well enough that the plain was criss-crossed with dry washes, gullies, arroyos, even deep gorges, twisting and mounting to the encircling rimrock. In the near distance clumps of mesquite, tiny green circles of bunchgrass near waterholes, small deserts with sun-whitened sand presented a breath-taking panorama stretching to the burning hills beyond.

Juano saw the prisoner fill his lungs with the sweet morning air, watched the grey-blue eyes sweep across the beauty of the land. Juano scowled.

'Look well upon this day, white man,' he whispered. 'You will not live to see another.'

* * *

'This is the place,' Green said.

They pulled their horses to a stop in a milling circle, the chalky dust sifting high. It was an open place, out in the middle of a wide sand flat, marked only by a huge boulder that had been swept down from the mountains to this site by the glacial torrents of pre-history.

Juano signalled the Texan to dismount, and stood watching him as he paced over to the rock and squinted up at the sun to get a bearing. Green aligned the mountain peaks on his right to his own satisfaction; then he paced out ten strides and halted, looking up.

'The guns are buried here,' he said.

At a rapped command from Juano, three warriors scuttled over to where Green stood and began to dig in the soft sand with their hands, chattering with excitement as they tossed the sifting grains aside like gophers. After a few minutes, one of them exclaimed gutturally, and Juano slid down from his horse's back and stalked quickly to where they crouched. A wooden crate lay with its top exposed; on the wood was stencilled in bold black capitals the words *Winchester Repeating Arms Company*. One of the warriors prised at the lid with a vicious looking throwing-axe. The lid lifted and fell back, revealing the shining rows of rifles glittering dully in the bright morning sun. Juano snatched one up and turned triumphantly to face Green.

'Guns here,' he said, his eyes glittering with greedy hate. 'Trade finished. Now—'

'Not quite!'

Something in the Texan's peremptory tone and confident stance told the Apache that there was yet more to hear. Puzzlement creased his cruel face.

'I ain't as stupid as yu seem to think, Juano,' Green told him. 'Them rifles is just so much scrap metal!'

An angry growl escaped Juano's lips; seeing the ire on their leader's face the other warriors came closer, ready for trouble.

'Does the white-eye seek a slow death?' raged Juano, spittle flecking his lips. 'Will he die like a crushed spider?' Green smiled slowly; and his coolness served to calm Juano, who saw that his loss of control in the face of the white man's calmness reflected discreditably upon him in front of his warriors. Gathering himself, the Apache spat: 'You will speak what you mean!'

'Afore I buried these rifles,' Green jerked his thumb at the box of weapons lying on its side in the sand, 'I took all the firin' pins out an' buried them somewheres else. Kind of an insurance policy, yu might say.'

For the first time since they had left the encampment, Manolito spoke. 'The white man has out-thought we Apache,' he said to Juano in his own language. 'See how he smiles as we fight like children for the shiny toys. Let us now honour the word of our people and let the white man go free with the woman.' Juano interposed with an angry gesture, but Manolito cut him off with a chopping motion of his hand. 'Enough!' he snapped. 'Your chattering wearies us all. Listen and learn!' Turning to the puncher, who had watched this exchange with keen interest, he put a question.

'How do they call you?'

'James Green,' replied the Texan.

'I think maybe we call you Coyote,' Manolito said.

'Coyote very clever.' Green nodded; the Apache was paying him a great compliment, for in their fireside stories, Coyote was the great crafty hero of Apache folklore. Manolito went on: 'Speak now. You will say what you want.'

Green nodded again. 'I'm takin' the girl now. We'll ride over yonder to that bluff.' He pointed out a promontory which could be seen about a mile away to the south. 'Yu an' yore warriors stay here until I signal like this.' He drew a white handkerchief from his pocket and waved it above his head. 'That'll mean I've dug up the firin' pins. Yu'll find 'em lying' on a rock out where they can be seen easy. Then I'll head south with the girl. Yu'll have yore guns.'

Juano stepped forward, rage firing his voice. 'The guns are mine,' he snarled. 'As the girl was mine, so are the guns. I do not share with Manolito!'

'Manolito does not ask for shares,' replied the Apache leader contemptuously. 'Keep your guns. Let us speak no more of it.' He turned again to face Green. 'You will do what you have said, Coyote? There will be no further games?'

'I'll do exactly what I told yu,' Green said levelly. 'Turn the girl loose an' we'll be ridin'.'

Manolito nodded. '*Enju*. Set the woman free.'

Barbara Davis was brought forward on the swaybacked plug which the Indians had furnished. Green knew that the animal would be unable to maintain a hard gallop for more than a few miles, but he was just going to have to take a chance on that. He had pushed his luck about as far as it would go; only their respect for Manolito held these warriors back now, and Juano would have blood in his eye the moment the Winchesters were assembled.

Manolito pointed to the south. 'Go now,' he commanded. Green raised a hand in a kind of salute. In a strange way he had come to feel almost a spirit of kinship for this proud

Apache. A glance to the side, however, revealed the ugly fact that Juano would never honour any bargain with a white man. Juano scowled at him.

'It's a dollar to a sick lizard he aims to nail my scalp to his wickiup wall come hell or high water,' Green told himself. 'Makes me glad I ain't fair-tradin' with him.' To the girl he said: 'Let's go.' Her eyes were wide with fear and disbelief. 'Just hold on tight an' don't look back,' he counselled. 'Ready?' She nodded, her lips tight. With a yell which caused several of the Apache ponies to shy violently, Green slapped his Stetson across Barbara's horse's ears, simultaneously booting Nigger into a gallop. They rocketed away down the sloping shelf and into the shallow valley, moving fast away from the watching Apaches. In a few moments more, the Indians could see them only as two small dots on the valley floor, a plume of rising dust marking their passage.

Green eased the pace once they were on level ground. The horses would require all their strength; he was sure that Juano would pursue with murder in his black Apache heart the moment the guns were finally assembled.

'Mr Green,' the girl shouted as they rode, her words whipped thin in the wind. 'Will you really give those savages rifles?'

Green grinned wolfishly. 'Gave my word, didn't I?' he shouted back. An expression of disgust touched Barbara Davis' face. 'So that they can kill more innocent people? What kind of man are you, anyway?'

'Not the kind yu figger!' Green yelled. 'I plugged the barrels of every gun in that crate! Now – ride!'

They reached the bluff on the far side of the valley, and Green reined the horses in. Dismounting, he rummaged beneath a rock and pulled out a flat cartridge box. He shook the box and the girl heard the metallic sound of the pins rattling inside it. Green smiled at her. 'Some o' them bucks is goin' to get a nasty shock when they pull the triggers o' them rifles,' he told her. 'Let's hope the fust one's Juano. Now: where ...' he was reaching further beneath the rock and pulled out now his own gunbelt, fastening it swiftly around his waist and snagging the holster ties snugly around his thighs.

'That feels a mite better,' he grinned. 'Now for the rifle.' He withdrew a Winchester from beneath the rock and slid it into the scabbard on his saddle. 'Mebbe Juano's bucks'll get a nasty shock if they come chasin' us,' he remarked. 'They won't be figgerin' on me bein' armed.'

Without waiting for her comment, he pulled out his bandanna and gave the prearranged signal to the Apaches. Almost immediately, they kicked their ponies into a run down the side of the valley, their shrill whoops sounding clearly in the still desert air.

Green was already in the saddle, and with the reins of his companion's horse tied firmly to his saddle pommel, led the way slightly west of due south, across the flat floor of the sandy plain, heading for the safety of Apache Wells, the old relay station on the Butterfield stage route. He glanced back at the girl as they thundered along. Her hair streamed out behind her head, and her eyes were narrowed against the rushing wind but she was riding proudly erect, and the cowboy sensed that for the first time she was savouring her freedom from her savage captors.

He pushed his lips out ruefully and urged Nigger to more speed. It was still a hell of a long way to Tucson.

CHAPTER SIX

As THEY surmounted another slowly rising incline, Green turned in his saddle. Far behind them, down the slope and across the flat plain they had travelled, his keen eyes discerned a rising dust cloud which could only mean one thing: Apaches! His mouth set in a grim line. So far they had kept the distance between the pursuing Indians and themselves about equal, but now the flanks of the girl's horse were soapy with lathered sweat. The animal was already beginning to labour, dragging on the reins tied to Nigger's saddle. Nor could they hope to out-distance the Apaches riding double. Nigger would run until his heart burst, but carrying a double load would slow even his ground-eating pace to one easily matched by the tough Indian mustangs. As these thoughts went through his mind, an exclamation escaped the girl, who pointed off to the west. To Green's astonishment another dust cloud could be seen, converging upon the route of the pursuing Apaches but concealed from them by a high ridge. A curse escaped the Texan's lips. Where had this second band of marauders sprung from? He shot another glance over his shoulder at the pursuing Apaches. 'Hell, they're gainin'!' he ground out. Then louder he shouted to the girl: 'Head for the rocks!' Off to their right was a jumble of boulders screened by bushes and sparse growths of cactus. It looked as good a place as any to make a stand. With the girl and the horses safely sheltered behind one of the biggest boulders, Green eased his sixguns in their holster and levered a shell into the breech of his Winchester. If they rushed him . . . he shook his head. He would accept this slender chance – any chance – rather than submit to capture, to slow and agonizing torture for himself and for the girl – God alone knew what.

His keen eyes slitted as the two arrowheads of dust converged. The long ridge dropped down to a point perhaps five hundred yards from where he lay with guns drawn. On the right the unknown newcomers raced headlong towards him; on the left thundered the Apaches. Both seemed still to be unaware of each other. Green settled his carbine to his shoulder, resolving to make every shot count.

Then: 'What in thunderation—?'

Without warning shots began to thunder out there on the plain. Green watched in amazement as two of the Apaches toppled from their horses. The war-party veered sharply to his left as the other band of riders came galloping into their path. Green saw now that they were white men, their guns blazing as fast as they could fire them. Their sheer firepower broke the Apache phalanx apart, driving the Indians off their line of attack. The sound of the gunfire was like the spattering of firecrackers as the white men – Green counted four of them now as they loomed closer – laid a deadly hail of lead upon the ranks of the wheeling Apaches. Green saw one of the Indians levering a bright new Winchester, and flinched instinctively as the Apache pulled the trigger. The gun exploded in the warrior's face, blowing him off the back of his horse, and there was a howl of rage from his fellow warriors at this evidence of Green's duplicity. The war party pulled away to the shelter of a deep gully and was lost momentarily to sight. The four riders thundered up towards the rocks and swung out of their saddles on the run, one of them gathering up the reins and hurrying the animals quickly behind the big boulders next to Green's horse. Throwing the reins about a branch, the man whirled and slid into a prone position alongside his fellows, who had all turned as they stopped moving, their rifles ready, facing the direction from which the Apache attack must come. There was a lull, however; the Apaches had been taught a sharp lesson and had no wish for another immediately. Green eased himself up and leaned his back against the boulder to survey his new-found companions.

They were an evil-looking bunch. The one facing Green looked up at him and grinned.

'How do,' he smiled, showing tobacco-stained teeth. 'Looks like we done saved yore bacon.'

'Which same I'm thankin' yu for,' Green replied. 'Shore lucky for me yu boys was out this way. How come yu was, anyway?'

'We been doin' some – huntin',' the man told him. He stuck out his hand. 'They call me Shiloh. Real handle's Dave. Dave Platt. From Fort Griffin, Texas.'

'I know it,' Green told him, affecting not to notice the proferred hand. Platt was dressed in greasy buckskins and a battered old Stetson with a long feather stuck in the band above the narrow brim. On his feet were Apache knee boots, and there was a long knife in an Apache sheath at his belt, as well as an Army Colt in a cutaway military holster. 'Half-breed' was Green's unspoken thought. 'An' a scalphunter to boot, or I miss my bet'. Aloud, he said: 'Green's my name, Jim Green. The young lady's name—'

'Hell, we know who she is,' Platt grinned evilly. 'Don't need to be no genious to work that out.'

Green tried a frown, although his heart sank a little at the halfbreed's words. 'I ain't shore I understand yu,' he said. 'Yu know her?'

'Yu trying' to kid me, Green?' snorted Platt. 'Half this goddamn territory is out lookin' for a blonde gal aged about eighteen took by the 'paches. We see yu skallyhootin' along ahead of a Cherry-cow warparty, towin' a blonde gal looks about eighteen – hell, it don't take much figgerin'.'

'Is she the Davis girl, mister?' asked the second of the group. This was a fresh-faced, wiry-looking youngster with a wide mouth and a nose that tended towards turning up. The boy had reddish-golden hair, and wore a shirt and denim pants, an eagle-bill Colt's .38 nestled in a snug holster on his left thigh. He looked out of place in this rough company, but Green reserved judgment. If, as was undoubtedly the case, these were four of the lawless breed Governor Bleke had told him about, then the boy's presence in the band was not encouraging. Green recalled that plenty of people had been misled by the baby face of William Bonney, alias Billy the Kid; but the Kid had been a killer, sure enough.

'Green, yu better git yore head down,' Platt warned, breaking in on his thoughts. 'Looks like yore friends yonder are fixin' to try us again. Quincy!' he raised his voice. 'Yu hear me?'

'Yo!' the man on the far side replied. Green could not see his face. The man was big, burly, roughly dressed. There were wicked-looking Mexican rowels on his scuffed boots. Green slid into a prone position and wiggled to where the girl sat with her back to a rock, protected from stray bullets.

'Mr. Green,' she said, trying to keep the fear out of her voice. 'Who are these men?'

'Well, they ain't Apaches,' he told her, trying to reassure her with a grin. 'That's in their favour. To tell yu the truth, ma'am, I'd make a deal with Satan hisself right now if he had rifles an' could pull a trigger.' He touched her shoulder. 'Don't yu worry none. Just keep yore head down when the shootin' starts.' She tried bravely to smile as he eased back to his position behind the boulders. As he did so a bundle on the saddlehorn of one of the horses caught his eye. A cold look of disgust settled on Green's face. There was no mistaking the grisly, dust-streaked trophies which hung there. They were scalps, Apache scalps.

'That shore is goin' to put the cat among the pigeons,' he muttered to himself. 'Them warwhoops ain't goin' to let us ride clear o' this country with scalps hangin' on our saddles. Damnation!'

The expletive came forcefully; accustomed as he was to the callous disregard for life on the frontier, the Texan had no brief for those who killed defenceless men and women for the bloody bounty of Mexico. Such men were the scum who poisoned the clear water of life. In other circumstances ... Green grinned wryly. 'Other circumstances is what I ain't in,' he told himself. 'I better get back.' He eased himself forward and took his place once more behind the big rock.

'How's the little lady?' asked Shiloh Platt, grinning evilly.

'All right,' Green said shortly, whereupon Shiloh slapped his thigh. 'That's purely fine,' he cackled. 'Got to look after the little lady – why she's worth her weight in gold!' He snickered at his own poor attempt at humour, and then the smile faded as the fourth man, a hulking fellow who had the build of a near giant, called 'Hyar they come!' and the Apaches came up out of the arroyo.

They were moving fast, but afoot now, well spread out to make the task of hitting them more difficult. The man called Quincy yelled 'Come an' get it, yu stinkin' savages!' and worked the lever of his rifle. They laid a heavy enfilade upon the approaching Apaches. One Indian was blasted off his feet in a whirl of limbs; another went down in a limp heap, as if his legs had melted. They drove volley after volley into the dodging, running warriors; two more whirled around and down in their death agonies. Bullets whispered over the heads of the defenders, and arrows flickered softly between the gaps in the rocks. A big buck leaped from his position behind a bush not twenty yards ahead, screaming his hatred, only to be torn apart by a hail of slugs before he had covered ten feet. A bullet slashed splinters of stone from the boulder in front of Shiloh Platt, who cursed as he shoved more cartridges into the gate of his Winchester.

Then swiftly, the Apaches melted into the ground and there was a long silence. After it, the staccato thunder of hoofbeats could be heard, and in a few seconds eight horses came galloping up the rise out of the arroyo, their riders curled like leeches around the horse's necks, on the blind side, guns blasting out to keep the heads of the defenders down. Rising like ghosts in the dust of their passing, the concealed warriors leaped to their feet, racing for the rocks ahead with killing frenzy extracting weird screams of rage from their corded throats.

To an uninterested spectator it might have looked impressive. In the blazing noon sunshine, the painted bodies of the Apaches shone like copper. The rumbling thunder of the galloping horses, and the screams of the incensed warriors mingled into an awesome sound as they hurled themselves upon the redoubt. It seemed inevitable that they must sweep over the tiny band and overwhelm them, but Green had signalled the quartet to hold their fire until he gave the word. The Apaches were like a bloodthirsty tidal wave not fifty feet away when the puncher yelled 'Fire!' and the point-blank volley blasted gaps into the oncoming line. As fast as they could lever their rifles the men fired, and then when the rifles were empty, they tossed them aside and drew their pistols – equally effective at such point-blank range. The murderous rain of death was irresistible, and the Apache line wavered, paused, and then broke. Those warriors still on their feet turned and ran for the sloping shelter of the arroyo, bullets pursuing them mercilessly as they fled. In another moment, all was silent. Only the thinning haze of powdersmoke remained to show that a battle had been fought; that, and the twisted bodies of the slain Apaches.

'Anyone hurt?' called Green.

'On'y them,' remarked Shiloh Platt callously, pointing his chin at the dead Indians. 'I count seven o' them out there.'

'How many was there to start with, mister?' the youngster asked Green.

'Sixteen, seventeen altogether,' Green told him.

'Then they been thinned down some,' Shiloh grinned. 'They won't be in no hurry to try hittin' us head-on again.'

'Yo're danged tootin',' the giant rumbled. 'Quince an' me got a couple o' them afore as well, didn't we, Quince?'

The bearded man edged over, still keeping a cautious eye on the empty flat in front of the rocks. Green now saw that Quincy was about thirty five, although he looked older because of a terrible scar which ran, livid and sickening, from the man's hairline, dividing his left eyebrow, down the cheek and into the heavily bearded jaw.

Dressed in dark blue pants, an old Army shirt, Quincy carried a heavy sixgun at his right hip, the inevitable Bowie knife sheathed as counterbalance on the left. Green frowned; the man's appearance was familiar and he racked his memory, trying to place the name: Quincy, Quincy. It wouldn't come. He listened as the bearded man spoke.

'We shore did, Tucson,' he told the giant. 'Two we nailed, an' seven out yonder makes nine out o' sixteen. I'd say they'll skedaddle.'

'Yo're right, Quincy,' called the youngster. 'They're pullin' out.'

It was true. The Apaches, strung out in an uneven line, were moving away from the scene of their defeat, but Green knew they would not go far away. As he watched, one of the Apaches detached himself from the line and turned in the saddle to shake a vengeful fist at the defenders in their rocky stronghold. It was Juano. His defiant gesture spoke as plainly as words: I have only lost a battle, not the war. Green pursed his lips.

From here on in, Juano would fight the true Apache way: skulking, ambushing, only attacking when the odds were in his favour. The puncher did not believe for a second that they were clear of the Chiricahuas yet. Shiloh Platt, however, was of a different viewpoint He slapped his thigh and gave vent to a whoop of joy.

Then placing his hand flat upon one of the boulders, he vaulted into the open, sliding the big knife from his belt, his eyes fixed upon the dead Apaches lying in the sun.

'Hold it right there!'

Shiloh wheeled as if he had been stung, while his three companions froze in their tracks. There was absolutely no mistaking the deadly menace in the words, and death was instinct in the stance of the man who had uttered them.

Shiloh's flickering eyes narrowed.

'Green?' he uttered. 'What th—?'

'If yo're aimin' to add to yore collection o' scalps, forget it!' was the rasping command.

Platt frowned, studying the man facing him properly for the first time. He had pegged Green as a cowpuncher who'd got lucky, but now the ice-cold grey-blue eyes, the crouching stance with the hands poised over the dull shining gun butts all indicated complete readiness to kill. Shiloh's eyes edged towards his companions. Quincy was regarding Green with an intent frown, as if seeking some memory in the puncher's face.

'Yore sidekicks might chip in, but yu'd still be dead, Shiloh,' Green said softly. 'Just do like I told yu an' ease on back in here.'

Still Shiloh Platt waited, silently weighing the situation. Green's words were chillingly final, but they could still be bluff. Maybe it was a good time to find out what calibre of man this Green was: gunman, or drifting cowpunch carrying two guns for added firepower in Apache country? Shiloh's instincts told him the former, but that half of him which was Mexican and darkly proud seethed with hatred at being ordered about, tested before those who followed him. His fingers moved slowly until they were curled above the gun at his side. Green made no movement, his eyes watching Shiloh with hawklike keenness, ready for any action from the half breed. Before the moment, tense and fraught, erupted into violence, Quincy's hoarse cry shattered the silence.

'Shiloh! Don't draw!' he cried. 'He's that Texas outlaw – Sudden!'

Sudden! Platt's eyes widened and a gasp of astonishment burst from his lips. He had nearly tried to draw on Sudden, the man whose reckless courage and deadly gunplay had already made his sobriquet a legend throughout the Southwest! His hand moved away from the butt of his gun as though it had suddenly grown red hot. Yet still the Texan stood, his cold gaze fixed unwaveringly on the half-breed.

'I told yu to get back in here,' he said flatly. Platt nodded, shaking himself into action. 'Shore, shore,' he mumbled, and although his heart seethed with hate, he did as he was bid. The Texan straightened up, the cold light still lying just behind his gaze, and faced Quincy. 'Yu know me?' he said.

'Shore I know yu, Sudden, an' yu know me. Fort Griffin, Texas. Sergeant Quincy, it was then.'

The memory flooded back. Now Green recalled the name, and the face, unscarred then and beardless. Quincy had been an Infantry sergeant in the Sixth Cavalry. He had been broken – expelled from the Army for excessive brutality, having nearly beaten a young recruit to death. The man's ungovernable rages had been more than even the rag-tag frontier Army was prepared to stomach. Quincy enraged was a mindless killer. They had crossed paths when Green had worked for a while as a scout for the Army; he had left without notice when a reward poster bearing his description had appeared on the notice-board outside the adjutant's office.

'Yu wasn't sportin' that scar when I seen yu last,' Sudden remarked to the scalphunter. 'What happened?' Quincy grinned evilly. 'All warwhoops don't part with their ha'r so willin', yu know,' he said. 'One played doggo – damn' near got me.'

He surveyed Green with some satisfaction, his hands placed akimbo on his hips. At this moment the girl came out from behind the rocks to join them.

'Well, girlie, come an' join us,' Quincy said with false heartiness in his voice. 'I was just sayin' to yore friend Sudden that now the Apaches has skedaddled, we oughta be movin' out o' here.'

'You are coming with us?' the girl asked, puzzled.

'Wouldn't dream o' lettin' yu cross this dangerous country all alone, girlie,' Quincy leered. 'Besides yore gunfighter friend here ain't so ungrateful as to not share the ree-ward with us after we done saved yore skins; now are yu, Green?' Shiloh said, with a meaning glance at the girl. 'We don't want nobody to get hurt, do we?'

'Yu better make yore meanin' good an' clear,' Sudden told him coldly, 'afore I lose my temper an' just naturally blow yore light out.'

'Blaze away, Sudden,' sneered Shiloh. 'Yu might get one of us, two even, but we'd get yu. Anyways, them warpaints is goin' to come back – I reckon yu oughta be glad o' some pertection. Yore best plan is to put up yore guns an' face fac's – yo're jest going to have to split that reward five ways.'

Before Green could answer, Barbara Davis pushed forward and planted herself in front of him. Her face was flushed with anger, and there were storm warnings in her pale blue eyes. 'What reward is he talking about?' she demanded.

'Yu mean – he ain't told yu, girlie?' Quincy said with disbelief in his voice. The girl shook her head

'I wasn't talking to you,' she snapped, stamping her foot. 'Mister Green, I demand to know!'

Shiloh stepped forward, smiling greasily. 'Why, lady, it looks like Mister Sudden here misled yu some. He ain't no knight in shinin' armour come to rescue the princess in the giant's castle, no ma'am. Yore daddy posted a reward o' five thousand dollars for yore return, an' Mister Sudden here was aimin' to hawg it all hisself, warn't yu, Jim?'

The Texan made no reply. Shiloh laughed and continued: 'He realized, however, he was makin' a mistake tryin' to outrun the 'paches on his lonesome. So he's hiring us as sorta bodyguards, make shore yu get home to yore daddy.'

He put a grimy hand on the girl's shoulder, and Barbara Davis pulled away, distaste evident upon her face. A flush mounted in Shiloh's face. Too good for the likes of him, was she? Well, there'd be time . . . He pasted the smile back on his face. 'Here, I ain't mindin' my manners none at all,' he said with forced jocularity. 'Shiloh's my monicker, Shiloh Platt. The giant there is called Tucson; don't answer to no other name. He ain't none too bright, but he's a big ox for shore, ain't yu, Tucson?' He cackled at his own poor joke.

'Aw, quit that, Shiloh,' Tucson rumbled. There was no real anger in his voice. He seemed to be accustomed to this kind of talk. 'The gent with the scar is called Quincy,' Shiloh went on. 'Good man with gun or knife or fists. Strong as a hoss. The kid there's called Rusty. Yu, Rusty, step over here an' say howdy to the lady.' The youngster shook his head, blushing slightly. 'Suit yoreself,' Platt said. 'He's kinda new to the game,' he explained. 'Yu'll have to excuse him.'

The girl shook her head in exasperation.

'Mister Green, will you please tell me what is going on? Why do these men keep calling you "Sudden"?'

'Why 'cause that's his nom-dee-ploom,' Quincy grinned, the side of his mouth twisted by the scar. 'Yore Mister Green is wanted for murder in Texas, girlie. Yu can bet the on'y reason he come after yu was to nail that ree-ward. Money means plenty to a man on the dodge.'

Barbara Davis looked at Sudden with deep contempt. 'I – I really thought – you were trying to help me,' she choked.

'Which I shorely was, ma'am,' the Texan said gravely.

'Oh,' I don't believe it!' she burst out.

'Never figgered yu would,' the Texan said quietly, as the girl went on: 'How can I trust you? Any of you?'

'All the same if yu do or yu don't girlie,' Quincy leered. 'Yo're stuck with us.'

'Don't yu worry none, lady,' the giant Tucson rumbled. 'We'll git yu back to yore daddy safe an' sound.'

'It's hard to believe you mean it,' the girl said tremulously. 'But you are right. I have no choice.'

'Attagirl, Barb-rie,' Quincy chuckled. 'Yu ain't likely to find nobody out here can give yu banker's references, an' yu can tie to that.'

At this remark the girl fell silent What the scar-faced man had said was only too true. If anyone were to outwit the Apaches it would be men like these, not the well-mannered young men with soft hands and voices who had called upon her at her father's ranch. These men were cruel, vicious, and rough; but it was a cruel and vicious land. She recalled in all its grim detail the scene in the ranch that night, after the Apaches had burst down the door of the bedroom, and . . . no, she would not think of that. Nor would she condemn men who killed the very beasts who had perpetrated the outrage. Barbara Davis was a frontier-bred girl, and of tough and durable ancestry. Her chin came up and a sparkle of pride touched her glance.

'Just take me home,' she said. 'My father will pay your ransom.'

Shiloh Platt grinned at these words and turned to face Sudden. 'Looks like yo're whipsawed, Sudden,' he jeered. 'Yu might as well make the best of it.'

'Yu won't mind if I take the "drag"?' was the sarcastic reply. It elicited a raucous burst of laughter from Quincy, who explained to the puzzled Tucson that the "drag" was a cattleman's term for the rear position on a trail drive. 'Mister Sudden's skeered we aim to shoot him in the back,' jeered Quincy.

'I don't blame him for that,' was Barbara Davis's cutting reply. It wiped the smirk off Quincy's face like a wet cloth taking chalk from a blackboard; dark rage suffused the scarred face for a moment; but Quincy controlled it.

Sudden was the only one to see the fleeting malevolence on Quincy's face, but he made no comment, content to file it away in his mind as another reason for not allowing the scarfaced scalphunter any rope at all.

'Less'n he wants some to hang himself with,' Green reflected with a mirthless smile. Aloud, however, he said: 'If we head out now we can get to Apache Wells afore dark. I'd as soon have adobe walls around me if they decide to take another crack at us.'

'Amen to that,' confirmed the youngster, Rusty, and he gave Green a friendly smile. Shiloh Platt nodded. Green was talking hard sense. Their supply of ammunition was not limitless, and another attack such as the one they had just survived might have a totally different ending if the Indians came back in full force.

'Tucson!' he shouted. 'Get the hosses; I'll lead out.' He turned to Sudden and there was a pure taunting malice in his snaggle-toothed grin. 'Yu take the rear, will yu, Sudden?' Roaring with laughter at his jest, he rode forward to join Quincy, and shook his head at a thought which came into it.

'Funny, Quince, I oughta be skeered o' the same thing Mister Sudden is: a bullet in the back. On'y I ain't. Now howd'yu figger that?'

Quincy said: 'I heard a lot about Sudden, but I never heard he was the backshootin' type.'

'Yu better be right,' Shiloh told him.

CHAPTER SEVEN

APACHE WELLS was one of the relay stations built by William Buckley and Silas St. John for the Butterfield Stage Line in the year 1858. Located near a plentiful spring of water, the Wells was a large stone building surrounded by a stone corral some forty-five feet long and fifty-five feet wide. It was situated on an open plain backing on to a high shelving slope; with the stage line long since defunct, it was used now as a stopping place for travellers and prospectors moving east to Apache Pass and old Fort Bowie, south to Tucson, or north-west to Phoenix.

The big old building stood sheltered in the shade of a grove of cottonwoods which Bill Buckley had planted when the station was first completed. The original building had been composed of a large central room with four rooms on each of its eastern and western sides; now, one wing was a pile of tumbled masonry coloured here and there with the faint green of a cactus which had found a fragile bed between the cracked stones. The windows of the station were little more than narrow slots, and had heavy plank shutters on the inside, loopholed for rifle or sixgun barrels. The building had withstood a hundred Apache raids in its time; if its walls could have spoken, what a tale they could have told – of the days of Cochise and Mangas Coloradas, of treachery and massacre and deceit!

The five men and the girl rode wearily up to the corral in the fading light, the horse's nostrils flaring as they scented the nearby water. The riders dismounted and slapped the dust from their clothes with their Stetsons.

Quincy led the way towards the dark doorway. He was detailing Tucson to take care of the horses when a shot thundered from one of the narrow window and his hat was whipped off his head by a heavy-calibre slug.

'What the—' Quincy's hand whipped down to the gun at his side; his piggy eyes sought the source of the shot.

'Stand still, thar!' came a creaky voice from within the building. Squinting his eyes against the poor light, Sudden could just descry the octagonal barrel of a Sharps' buffalo rifle poking through one of the slit windows. Before he could speak, Quincy's voice boomed out:

'Hold yore fire, damn yu – we're white men!'

'Step into the light whar I can see ye!' came the uncompromising reply. A shutter swung back and the lamplight inside the building spread across the yard, throwing the figures standing there into bold relief. After a moment, the rifle barrel was withdrawn and they heard the rusty door-bolts squeaking as they were laboriously drawn. An old man, his snowy hair shining like a halo in the lamplight, stood on the porch; the rifle was ported warily across his arm, ready to be swung into instant action if need be.

Quincy spread his hands in a reasoning gesture.

'Take it easy, old-timer,' he said. 'You c'n see we ain't Injuns.'

'Got ye an Injun squaw thar, ain't ye?' snapped the man. 'I don't hold none with stealin' 'pache wimmin . . .'

'Naw,' Quincy said, 'yo're off-beam, mister. She's a white gal we took off the warwhoops in trade.'

'Hmph,' the old man grunted, not altogether convinced.

'Yu own this place?' Shiloh asked, 'or are yu going to stand aside an 'let us come in?'

'Whyfor yu throw a shot at me, anyway?' Quincy said in an aggrieved tone. 'Yu could see we wuz white, couldn't yu?'

'I c'd see white-men's clothes,' the old man replied 'Hit wouldn't be the fust time a few Chiricahuas rigged theirselves up in store clothes to git near to a house. Hit don't hurt none to be shore. Yu don't get no second chanct with them red divils.'

'We jest had a run-in with a war-party our own selves, mister,' Rusty said. 'The young lady is mighty peaked, so if yu—'

'Hell, o' course, o'course! Don't jest stand there, dammit! Bring 'er in, boy! Bring er in!'

They followed him into the station, entering a huge square room. Down one side of it ran a counter that had obviously been a bar at one time; at the end furtherest from the door was an area filled with broken-down chairs and tables where in former days travellers on the stagecoach had dined. An old cast-iron range still stood in one corner; it had proven too strong for either the Apaches or the weather to break. The old timer had kindled a cherrywood fire in it against the growing chill of the night. The smell of coffee filled the dust-mantled room.

'Eady's m'name,' the old man told them. 'Tobias Eady. I do a leetle prospectin' hereabouts.'

Rusty looked at the man as though he had declared his ability to fly. 'Yu – do what?' he choked. 'Don't yu know these mountains is crawlin' with hostiles?'

'Shore,' Eady said unrepentantly. 'I tries to pacify 'em if I meets up with any.' He leaned over and patted the shining stock of the Sharps', and ran a forefinger down the serrated row of notches neatly sliced into it. 'They leave me alone, I leave them alone,' he finished. 'Otherwise, Betsy hyar discourages 'em a mite.' He shook his head, laughing softly to himself, and shuffled over to the stove, the red coals throwing a warm glow on his worn, but clean buckskins. 'Yu boys got any grub, I'll be happy to cook it fer ye,' he offered. 'Yo're shore welcome to share m'cawfee.'

'Thanks a lot, Eady,' Green said, stepping forward and speaking for the first time since they had entered the station. He had been carefully assessing its defences and had noted with satisfaction that the building was still capable of resisting all but the most overwhelming onslaught. 'I better call off some names to go with the faces yu see. I'm Jim Green. The young lady's name is Davis. Barbara Davis.' He paused to see if the name registered in any way, but Eady evinced not a flicker of interest. 'The kid's called Rusty – which yu'd figger with that mop o' red hair,' Green went on with a grin. 'Tucson is the big feller. The other two is Quincy an' Platt.'

Eady nodded disinterestedly; he was preoccupied with his chores. Once he looked up and said to the girl: 'They's plenty water if yu feel like washin', missie. Won't take but a minnit to hot yu some up.'

'Oh, that would be grand,' exclaimed Barbara enthusiastically. 'I feel so – dirty.'

'Wal, 'paches ain't the world's cleanest critters,' agreed the old man, pouring some water into a big iron cauldron, which he swung on a metal rod across the fire. 'You can use one o' the rooms on the west side,' he told the girl. 'They's still purty well intact, although yu might have to share 'em with a spider or three.' The lined face creased in a mischievous grin, and a faint smile appeared in response upon the girl's tired face. 'Why yo're right purty when yu smile,' Eady remarked. He swung the iron rod away from the fire, lifting the cauldron clear. 'One o' yu boys want to heft thisyere water over into a side room for the missie?'

Rusty stepped forward and without a word lifted the cauldron, staggering across the room with it to a doorway on the far side. Kicking open the door of the room, he went in; the girl followed docilely, and as she did, Shiloh Platt turned to Quincy.

'Quince,' he said. 'Yu watch things. I'm aimin' to make shore the gal don't get no fool ideas about escapin' . . . I'll keep an eye on her.'

The emphasis upon these last words left no doubt as to his intentions, and Quincy grinned evilly.

'Shore, Shiloh,' he agreed. 'She's a purty—'

'Shiloh!'

The half-breed wheeled, surprise written large upon his face; for the challenge had come from an unexpected quarter. Half-expecting interference from Sudden, Shiloh found himself unprepared when the cutting voice of the kid, Rusty, stopped him in his tracks. He turned slowly, his hands well in sight and still. Rusty was standing with feet planted apart, directly between Shiloh and the doorway of the room into which Barbara Davis had gone.

'What is this?' Shiloh growled.

'Yu know what it is, Shiloh!' snapped Rusty. 'Yu ain't goin' anywhere near her.'

'Is that so?' gritted Shiloh. 'An' who's going to stop me?'

'I am!' Rusty said, flatly. 'If yu aim to put a hand on that doorknob, yo're goin' to have to step across me to do it, an' yu can tie to that!'

Shiloh caught Quincy's eye, and the scarfaced ex-soldier began to ease slowly along the bar, intending to move into a position where he and Shiloh could whipsaw the boy. He had moved no more than a few inches when Sudden remarked in almost a conversational tone, 'If yu take another step, Quincy, yo're liable to fall an' hurt yoreself.' Quincy stopped moving, darting a glance of hatred at the lounging figure across the room. But there was no mistaking the threat in Sudden's words and Quincy was not fool enough to ignore them. Old Eady watched the tableau with wide eyes, while Tucson, who had gone out in back to fetch some food from the saddlebags, stood stock still in the half-open doorway.

Shiloh had not missed Sudden's quiet remark, and knew that if he started the ball, he would not be able to rely on Quincy; at the first hostile move, Sudden would cut him down. The kid was fast enough with his gun, that Shiloh knew; but even if he took him, there would still be that coldly-smiling Texan to face. No, a lascivious look at the girl was not worth this kind of trouble; Shiloh knew that the odds were wrongly stacked, and he shrugged. 'Hell, Rusty, no call to get all hotted up. Whose side yu on, anyway?'

'I didn't know we'd chosen sides,' the boy remarked, 'but if we have, I'm on the girl's an' that's whatever.'

'Good for you, sonny,' crowed Eady. 'That's tellin' 'im.'

Deep rage burned inside Shiloh at this, he felt, unwarranted intrusion by one of his own band, but he let none of this show. He did not intend to face a showdown on anything except his own terms.

'Yu an' me is goin' to have a quiet talk one o' these days,' he scowled.

Rusty shrugged and turned away. 'Fine,' he said offhandedly. 'I'll see if I can think o' some interestin' things to say.'

Shiloh grunted, still seething inside at this cavalier treatment. He turned his attention upon Tucson, who still stood in the open doorway.

'Yu goin' to stand there all night, yu dumb ox?' he screeched. He whirled on Eady. 'An' yu – ain't you got nothin' to do except gawp? How long d'yu aim to be with that grub?'

'About as long as she takes,' snapped Eady. 'I won't be done no quicker on account o' yu jabberin'.'

Shiloh stamped across the room, snatching the saddlebag out of Tucson's unresisting hands. He rummaged in it, and not finding what he wanted, snapped 'Go an' look in the other saddlebag – there's some whisky in it.'

Tucson frowned at Shiloh's tone. 'I ain't no servant, Shiloh,' he grumbled.

'Oh, get the bottle, yu stupid ox!' Shiloh cursed. 'I ain't got all night.'

Eady looked at Sudden meaningfully. 'Yore friend's got a mean tongue,' he remarked quietly.

'He shore has – although he ain't no friend o' mine,' the Texan told him. Eady nodded absently, and went on with frying the slices of bacon he had cut from the hunk that Tucson had brought in. Sudden watched Shiloh and Quincy slouched at the broken-down bar; they were whispering quietly. Sudden recalled Eady's remark about Shiloh's outbursts. 'Mebbe his tongue's goin' to trip him up afore long,' he thought as he watched Eady putting the food on to the tin plates. 'Mebbe it'll be to my advantage.'

* * *

Supper was eaten in a desultory silence. Barbara had joined them, and her skin glowed pinkly from the scrubbing she had given it. Her hair was bright golden in the lamplight, cleansed of the dirt which had formerly matted it, and her pale blue eyes, firm full lips, and short, straight nose made the men at the table aware that the girl was beautiful. More than once Sudden caught Rusty's eyes upon the girl, watching her adoringly; he saw the boy flush deeply when Barbara's cool blue eyes met his directly on one of these occasions. The Texan noted the gleam in the eyes of Shiloh Platt, who feasted his gaze upon the girl's slim form. Even Tucson was moved to a clumsy gallantry, holding the rickety chair for the girl as she rose from the table after the meal.

Rusty came over to speak to Sudden. 'The girl's purty tired, Green,' he said. 'She needs rest. Lots o' sleep.'

'I know it,' Sudden told him. 'She's had a rough ride, but we ain't out o' the woods yet.'

'Yu know – Shiloh ain't plannin' on sharin' that reward with yu!' burst out Rusty.

Sudden nodded. 'He ain't the sharin' kind – although I'm shore obliged to yu for mentionin' it.' His smile, the boy noted, made the Texan's whole face look younger. He thought he could like a man like this a whole lot. Sudden asked him a question, breaking in on Rusty's reverie.

'How come yo're mixed up with Shiloh Platt, Rusty? Yu don't look like no scalphunter to me.'

Rusty's face went bitter. 'Yu got to look like a scalphunter to be one?' He shook his head as if in answer to his own question. 'I'm bettin' yu know better'n most how little difference it makes what a man's done an' what he gets labelled with havin' done.'

The grim look on the Texan's face confirmed the accuracy of this remark, moving Rusty quickly to contrition. 'Hell, Jim – I never—'

'O' course not,' Green smiled. 'There's times I forget it for days at a stretch.' He changed the subject. 'Yu want to tell me how yu got mixed up with Shiloh?'

Rusty shook his head, a dogged stubbornness creeping into his expression. 'I got to work her out, Jim . . .' He shot a miserable glance at the girl. 'That's if it ain't too late awready.' Sudden had intercepted the look at Barbara Davis, and it confirmed his suspicion that the boy was regretting whatever circumstances had driven him into his present company. However, he did not press the younger man. 'If yu want to talk about it sometime, yu let me know,' was all he said. 'I got a feelin' yu don't like Shiloh Platt no more'n I do.'

'Like him?' hissed Rusty. 'I hate his guts!' He stalked away without another word and went over to the far corner of the room, where he sat moodily in a chair, with his chin on his hand, looking into nothing.

Sudden was still pondering the boy's outburst when they all rolled into their blankets for the short sleep which was all they would allow themselves. The odds were on a dawn attack; every one of them must be awake and ready long before sunup.

Sudden opened an eye to peer at Quincy, who had taken the first watch. The scarfaced scalphunter was a strange mixture: one moment jaunty, almost likeable; the next, an insane and uncontrollable killer. Shiloh, Tucson, Rusty: they were an unlikely crew. Wondering what strange twists of fate had led them to join forces, Sudden fell into a healthy sleep, his last thought it might be a long time before he had another as peaceful.

CHAPTER EIGHT

At dawn the Apaches, their copper skins daubed with vivid colours, their faces painted black, slithered over the rim of a gully on the southern side of the relay station and wormed forward, using every scrap of cover, towards the shelter of the stone corral wall.

Inside the station they waited ready; each man had been allotted a window position, and Barbara Davis sat at a table, boxes of cartridges in front of her, ready to reload the guns that the defenders would thrust into her hands as they emptied them.

'Keep yore aim low,' Sudden counselled them all, in a whisper. 'It don't matter where we hit 'em, as long as it stops 'em comin'.'

Rusty nodded grimly at these words. His eyes strayed across the room towards Barbara, who met his gaze with an open, friendly smile. Of all her companions, the girl thought, the one called Rusty was by far the nicest. It seemed impossible that he could be involved in Shiloh Platt's filthy occupation.

'Here comes one now,' came Shiloh's sibilant whisper. 'Shall I nail 'im?'

'Hold yore fire!' rasped Sudden. 'We want to take as many as we can on the first volley. They don't know we're waitin' for 'em.'

'He's sneakin' close to the well,' Shiloh said. 'I'm afeared he's goin' to drop some pizen in it.'

'Warhoops use that water as much as white folks, mister,' Eady said quietly. 'They won't pizen it.' He eased his head close to the window and peered around the edge. 'Any minnit now one o' them'll stand up long enough to draw a shot,' he warned. 'Don't nobody be tempted: 'paches allus figger better to risk one warrior than the whole war party.'

'If he gets too close in drop 'im anyway,' Quincy growled.

The bearded man turned back to his window, then sighed. 'Aha,' he said. 'Hyar's a couple more.'

'Two on this side as well,' hissed Eady from the west wall, his big rifle ported ready.

Sudden risked a quick glance around the edge of the window and saw three braves worming across the yard on their bellies. This was it. 'Let 'em have it!' he yelled, and the guns blasted their murderous crossfire out of the windows. With howls of demented rage at this perfidy, the Apaches leaped to their feet, running like deer for cover; all except one, who hurled himself headlong towards the window on the west wall. He was smashed off his feet by a bullet from Eady's buffalo rifle, the .50 calibre slug hurling him in a broken heap some yards to the side. The old man touched a finger to his tongue, and tapped the smoking end of his rifle barrel with it. Then he calmly proceeded to slice a notch out of the butt with his knife, ignoring the hail of shots which was now directed at the house by the rest of the war-party behind the corral. Now that their sneak attack had failed, the Apaches devoted their hatred and energy to pouring fusillade after fusillade into the window apertures in the hope that one of the leaden messengers would find a random destination. Spouts of splintered stone spanged from the walls as the bullets slashed into the house; some chunks of wood were torn from the board shutters which blocked the narrow windows.

'Keep down!' Quincy yelled, although the advice was at best superfluous.

'Blaze away, dear hearts,' crooned Eady. 'Yu'll need more'n rifle slugs to make a dent in these walls.'

The defenders crouched low as the barrage slackened. It could hardly last long. In the first place the Apaches did not have the ammunition to sustain it. And the second more chilling reason was that this was not the Apache way of fighting.

Sudden risked a glance out of the window. At some distance beyond rifle range he could see a group of Apaches on horseback. They were pointing at the house and gesticulating furiously.

'What they up to, Green?' called Shiloh. 'C'n yu see anythin'?'

'They're palaverin' on a bluff over yonder,' the Texan told him.

'Mebbe askin' the Everywhere Spirit for advice,' Eady cackled.

'They shore ain't havin' a sewin' bee, anyways,' grunted Quincy. Even as he watched, the arguing band of Apaches separated and disappeared into the gully beyond the corral wall. In a few moments there was complete silence, and the watchers in the beleaguered station waited tensely for any hint of the next Indian move. None came. The sun rose higher and the heat grew, but all remained still outside.

'Yu figger mebbe they've just rid off an' given up?' Shiloh asked, his tone betraying his lack of any such belief.

'Yu could allus slide out an' take a gander,' Rusty grinned. 'If they kill yu, we'll know they ain't gone yet.'

'Very funny,' sneered Shiloh. He turned to Eady. 'Yu got plenty o' water in here, old man?'

'Enough,' Eady said. 'Unless yo're talkin' about a long stay. Seven o' us could git through a powerful lot o' water if them red divils decided to wait us out.'

'Hell's teeth!' swore Quincy 'Yu mean if they decide to jest sit out there, we're a-goin' to run out o' water?'

'Not right away,' the old man said, his eyes glinting with scorn. 'Don't yu get yoreself all frighted, now, Quincy.'

'Yu watch yore lip,' Quincy threatened darkly.

'Yu reckon they'll try an' sit us out, Jim?' Eady asked Sudden, ignoring the taciturn Quincy.

'They might,' the Texan conceded. 'My guess is they'll take another crack at us afore they decide on it.'

'My feelin's,' agreed the oldster. 'Apaches gits a mite impatient sometimes. It can be the death o' them . . .' He grinned toothlessly and patted the serrated stock of his rifle.

The thought of escape was still running through Shiloh Platt's head like a ferret through a rabbit warren.

'Mebbe we could wait until dark, an' make a run for it!' he suggested.

'Yu want to try, fly at it,' Sudden told him cuttingly. 'Yu won't mind if we hang back an' watch how yu make out?'

His sardonic words silenced the half-breed, who gnawed at his lips. Quincy broke the silence.

'Take no mind o' Shiloh,' he grinned. 'He jest nacherly hates bein' cooped up. I reckon he knows well enough there ain't a chance o' gettin' through that war-party with his hair in one piece.'

'Not yet there ain't,' Eady confirmed. 'We got to jest hold on an' see what happens next.'

Sudden turned his gaze on the girl, who sat where she had scrambled, in the corner, when the hail of bullets had been smashing into the house. 'Yu all right ma'am?' he asked. Barbara Davis's chin came up.

'Don't concern yourself, Mister Green,' she replied, her voice cold. 'I am still intact. Your reward money is in no danger.'

Shiloh cawed with laughter. 'That's tellin' him, sister,' he cawed. 'Damn my eyes if yu ain't the li'l spitfire for shore!'

Rusty bristled at Shiloh's words. 'Keep yore tongue civil, Platt!' he rasped. 'Or I'll—'

'You'll what?' growled Shiloh, his good humour evaporating.

Before the youngster could reply, Sudden spoke in a mild voice. 'Fightin' among ourselves ain't goin' to help,' he remarked.

Not a man among them was misled by the gentle tone. 'Keep yore eyes peeled on that yard. Any o' them 'paches sneaks up to a window, an' the man guardin' it'll be a goner shore.'

Shiloh Platt wheeled back to his window, as if afraid that during the brief in his vigilance an Indian had in truth wormed up to the window, and even now lurked there, grinning, his rifle cocked.

'Somethin' happenin' over on this side,' Tucson announced. 'I see dust behind the wall.'

Sudden motioned Rusty to cover the window he had vacated and moved quickly across to Tucson. He peered gingerly out of the window, marking the spot which the giant indicated. 'That ain't dust,' he said finally. 'It's smoke. They're buildin' a fire out there.'

'Now what in hell—?' Quincy began wonderingly.

Almost as if in answer to his question, three fire arrows arched upwards from behind the wall, climbing steeply with smoke trailing behind them, then dropping down to thunk viciously into the roof overhead. Sudden looked a question at Eady, who answered it with a grin.

'They ain't goin' to have much luck with that ol' dodge,' the old man cackled 'Fellers what built this place knowed their business: roof's solid stone with sand piled atop of it to keep the heat out. About as much chance o' their settin' it afire as there is o' Quincy here gettin' into Paradise.' His shoulders heaved with silent laughter at his grim humour.

The defenders heard the rain of fire-arrows, for such it now became, thunking into the roof above their heads and, despite Eady's reassurance, waited tensely for any hint that the flames might have caught; but none came. After a while, it became obvious that the Indians had realized the ineffectiveness of this method of attack. The whistle of arrows ceased, and Eady looked around triumphantly.

'Told ye there was nothin' to worry about,' he said. 'Boys what built Apache Wells knowed a few Injun tricks their ownselves.'

Again the silence fell, and the hush invaded the beleagured station. The sun had climbed to its zenith now, and struck down upon the parched land with merciless ferocity. The sky was as blue as a Chinaman's robe, without the hint of a cloud in all its brazen expanse. Nothing stirred; no bird sang. It was as if Nature herself had ordered all of her creatures away from this place of death, leaving it empty, desolate and forbidding. Another hour crawled past, and then another, and still the silence reigned. Guns cocked and ready, the defenders waited.

CHAPTER NINE

'You aren't like – the others,' Barbara Davis said quietly to Rusty. They sat together at a table, eating the cold meat that was their only food. Sudden had insisted upon advantage being taken of the lull in the onslaught.

'No tellin' when they'll hit us again,' he had said. 'It makes sense to grab somethin' to eat while the goin's good.'

None of them, not even Rusty himself, had remarked that Sudden's organization of the breaks had resulted in the boy's being left alone with Barbara Davis, but Sudden's plan had been deliberately effected. 'If that kid's a wrong 'un then I'm gettin' old an' oughta be put out to pasture,' he had told himself. 'Me'bbe if he talks to the girl . . .' Thus the two sat together now, Barbara looking earnestly at her young companion. Rusty looked up at her words and hope fled across his face, leaving bitterness in its wake. 'Shore I am,' he said finally. 'Yu can't touch pitch—'

'And not be defiled? Oh, Rusty, that's nonsense and you know it,' she insisted. 'I cannot bring myself to believe that you—' She stopped, unable to bring herself to complete the rest of her sentence.

'That I done my share o' scalphuntin', yu was goin' to say,' he said. 'Well, yo're right about that, at least. I never lifted no 'pache hair, but I reckon that ain't no excuse. I'm one o' them an' that's that.'

'Won't you tell me how you came to be mixed up with this dreadful band?' the girl asked. The concern in her voice thrilled him, although he shifted uncomfortably in his chair in the hope that she would fail to see his reaction.

'Yu really want to know?'

'I really want to know, Rusty.'

The young man's face was serious as he recounted the events which had led him into this present company. It was not a very original story; a rancher's daughter, Barbara Davis had heard it, or variations upon it, many times in her life. The young puncher, his monthly pay burning a hole in his pocket goes into the nearest town to spend it as fast as possible. Full of rotgut whisky, he finds himself in a saloon, half drunk at a gaming table, betting steadily and losing every hand.

'Shoulda knowed, if I'd had a lick o' sense, that cardsharp was a-usin' a stacked deck. But I jest kept on plungin' an' in the end, when I was down to my last chip, the gambler makes a slip an' I see him cold-deckin' me. I call him, an' he goes for his gun. I get mine out faster an' he goes down. These two strangers grab me an' hustle me out o' there. They tell me the law don't take kindly to its citizens bein' salivated. They tell me they're leavin' town for a long trip in the mountains, an' need an extra hand what's useful with a gun. I ain't got much choice, so I ride with them.'

'They were—?'

'Quincy an' Shiloh, that's right,' he confirmed. 'They offered me a deal. If we made any money prospectin' – that's what they tol' me at first – they'd take my share an' square the law in Bisbee. Then I'd be free an' clear. They was rough, but I wasn't in no spot to be choosy, so I rode along. Tucson was waitin' for them outside o' town. I believed the pair o' them about goin' prospectin' in the Dragoons. What a fool!' he cursed. 'I never knowed then what they was aimin' to go prospectin' for.'

Barbara gasped at this. 'You discovered that they were – bounty hunters?'

'Call 'em what they are: scalphunters,' he gritted. 'Yeah, I found it out. They come into camp one night, Quincy an' Shiloh, Apache scalps hangin' on their saddles. I faced 'em with it, said I wasn't aimin' to ride with no scalplifters an' they laughed at me. "Pull out if yu've a mind," Shiloh tol' me. "Yu won't get a mile on yore own. The Injuns has yu spotted for one of us, an' they'll treat yu accordin'." ' The boy shrugged. 'I had to admit he was right. I wouldn't have had no chance alone. So I promised myself I'd cut loose o' them the minnit we got to Tucson again, give myself up an' take the consequences. We was headin' south when we seen yu an' Green runnin' ahead o' that Chiricahua war-party.'

'Green,' she said with a tiny grimace. 'He's no better than that – that half breed!'

'I ain't so shore,' Rusty told her. 'I heard o' plenty o' men with Sudden's kind o' reputation gettin' crimes pinned on them they never done.'

'How can you defend him?' she asked in amazement. 'He is a murderer, wanted by the law!'

'So'm I,' he reminded her flatly.

She shook her head. 'It isn't the same, Rusty; don't deny it. The name of Sudden is synonymous with gunfighting and killing.'

'Mebbe,' Rusty admitted. 'Allasame, I can't picture him murderin' defenceless Injuns for their scalps like Quincy, nor enjoyin' it like Shiloh Platt. Nope, Bar— Miss Davis, I mean—' he stopped in confusion. The girl touched his hand shyly. 'Barbara is fine, Rusty,' she told him.

'Wal – Barbara,' Rusty hoped the gulp was soundless. 'I was goin' to say: if we got any chance o' gettin' out o' this alive, I'm bettin' it's Jim who's going to pull it off.'

'You like him, don't you?' she said, wonderingly.

'I reckon he's square,' Rusty told her. 'But even if he ain't, I want yu to know one thing: I'll do the best I can to see yu come to no harm.'

The girl bent her head, a slow flush mounting to her cheeks.

To cover her confusion, she stammered 'I want you to know – I believe you, Rusty. About why you had to join up with Platt, and what happened in Bisbee. When we get back—' Her voice faltered for a moment, and she said despairingly, 'Oh, Rusty do you think we shall ever reach Tucson alive?'

'Shore we will,' he said, trying to put an assurance into his words that he was far from feeling.

* * *

Eady broke the silence.

'Yu boys ain't told me yet huccome yo're ridin' in these parts anyways.' When neither Quincy nor Shiloh replied he asked a question of Sudden: 'Yu boys allus ride together?'

The Texan shook his head. 'We ain't together,' he said flatly.

'Jest – teamed up,' added Shiloh Platt, and then: 'Yu found any gold up in the mountains, Eady?'

'Enough to eat with,' was the terse reply. 'How long yu boys been scalphuntin'?'

The air went electric at these casual words from the old timer, who watched their reactions carefully as he spoke them. Quincy broke the tension with a harsh laugh.

'Dunno what yo're talkin' about,' he said. 'We ain't scalphunters, we're prospectors. Like yu, old timer.'

'Yu ain't like me an' don't yu ever think hit,' Eady snapped. 'An' don't think I'm so old I gone blind. I seen the scalps on yore saddles. Yu ain't no more prospectors than I'm the king o' China.'

Shiloh rose lazily from his chair by the window 'Okay,' he said softly. 'So we're scalphunters. So what, yu ol' goat?'

The old man shrugged. 'I jest wanted to sort things out in my haid,' he replied. 'Yu boys oughta know that the 'paches don't take kindly to scalphunters. Yo're bad luck in this country, an' that's sartin. If we get out o' this bilin' yu boys brung with yu, I'm servin' yu notice: I'll be cuttin' loose. I don't want to be within ten miles o' yu if them Cheery-cows ketch yu.'

'They ain't goin' to ketch us, old man,' sneered Shiloh. 'Yu can bet yore boots on that.'

'Hit ain't my boots; it's my skin what's up for grabs,' retorted the grizzled oldster unabashed. He turned to face Sudden. 'Yu ain't exackly over-talkin' yoreself,' he observed. 'Yu another o' this breed?' He jerked a contemptuous thumb at Shiloh.

'Mister Green is an adventurer,' Barbara Davis interposed, overhearing the question as she and Rusty rose from the table. Rusty laid a restraining hand upon her arm, but she shook it off, without anger. 'You probably know him by his better-known name: Sudden.'

Eady whistled. 'So . . . yo're Sudden, are yu? I heard a lot o' tales about yu,' he told the Texan. 'Some good; some not so good. Usually operate alone, don't yu?'

'He operates wherever the money is best, I'm sure,' Barbara Davis said with an edge in her tone. Eady nodded absently, a frown creasing his brow. Sudden felt that the old man sensed something amiss, some hint of the tension between Sudden and the scalphunters, but before he could speak, Shiloh Platt yelled 'Here they come!' and levered a stutter of shots out of his window.

The men leaped for their positions like well-trained troops, their guns scything a hail of bullets across the yard. The Apaches had sneaked up to the corral wall and then, *en masse*, vaulted it and were running flat out for the house heads down, as if ignoring the very presence of the deadly guns.

'They been makin' medicine,' Sudden shouted. 'They figger they're bulletproof. Prove 'em wrong!'

His twin sixguns laid down a withering arc of fire from the window at which he stood, blasting out in what sounded like a continuous staccato explosion. Quincy's Winchester, the booming roar of Eady's buffalo gun, the sharper bark of the sixguns, all mingled with the whirr of deadly arrows and the hiss of slugs, the shrill Apache yells, combining in a hell of sound that deadened the eardrums and suspended time, stifling the brain until the hands fired the hot guns as if motivated by clockwork, the stiff arms lifting the weapons automatically.

Again the Apaches fell back, their charge stopped dead in its tracks. There were seven more sprawled bodies in the corral outside.

'Jest look at that, will yu,' Quincy exclaimed. 'There's five hundred simoleons a layin' out there in the sun jest a-waitin' to be collected.'

'Go on out an' collect, then,' Shiloh grinned.

'Thank yu kindly,' Quincy said. 'Business is jest a mite confinin' at the moment.'

'Yu got more brains than I give yu credit for,' Eady remarked idly, drawing a black look from the scar-faced one. 'Hush, what's that?'

They listened but could hear nothing. Tucson said as much.

'Hell, yu wouldn't a' heard it if the Dragoons fell down,' Eady snorted contemptuously. 'I thought I heard horses.'

'They could be pullin' back,' Sudden guessed.

'Bah,' exclaimed Shiloh Platt. 'Yo're dreamin'.'

Again the silence fell. An hour stole away and then another.

No sounds came from outside, and after a while they heard a bird twitter. Eady looked at Sudden and cocked an eyebrow.

'That ain't no Injun,' he observed.

Had the Apaches truly gone? Had the punishing defeat made them give up in disgust and return to their stronghold? The Texan felt sure that Juano would not allow them to leave this land with so many of his warriors dead. He edged to the window. The twilight was stealing up from the deeper shadows of the arroyo like a sneak-thief.

'Yu think they've skedaddled, Jim?' Rusty asked.

'I reckon not,' was the reply. 'But there's on'y one way to make shore.' Without another word, Sudden eased himself over the window sill, and before any of them could stop him, he had vanished into the death-still silence beyond the empty corral.

CHAPTER TEN

TWENTY minutes later, Sudden was back inside the house, brushing the clinging dust from his clothes as everyone clustered around, their faces eager for news of what he had seen.

'They ain't gone,' he announced. 'They're down by the crick bed over yonder, mebbe quarter of a mile. I could see the belly-fires. Couldn't get too close, but I heard enough to know they ain't pleased with theirselves. They're fillin' their bellies with *tiswin* to get theirselves fired up again for tomorrow.'

His listeners looked grim at this depressing news. Rusty reached out to touch Barbara Davis's hand, and this sympathetic gesture brought a shy smile to her face.

'That's bad news, Sudden,' Quincy rumbled. 'We can't hold out indefinite.'

'My thoughts exackly,' the Texan said. 'Which is why we're goin' to make a run for it.'

They looked at the smiling puncher as if he had miraculously grown a second pair of arms. Shiloh Platt put their feelings into astonished words: 'Yu loco, Sudden?'

'Yu ain't gettin' me out there with them bucks pirootin' around full o' cactus juice,' added Quincy. 'I'm kinda attached to my hair.'

'Then keep it on an' lissen,' was Sudden's economical comment. 'If we stay here, one o' two things is bound to happen: either we run out o' water, which'd be bad enough, or wuss – we'll run out o' bullets.'

There was a chilled silence. Sudden's even assessment of their predicament was an accurate one, and it took little enough imagination to picture what would happen to them if the Apaches had the station still surrounded when all the ammunition had gone.

'Hell, mebbe we c'n wait 'em out,' Shiloh said.

'An' mebbe we can't,' Eady added. 'Green's right; we're boxed an' them red divils know it. All they gotta do is wait. And they'll do it.' He turned to Sudden. 'What's yore idea, Green?'

'It's a long shot,' Sudden replied. 'An' mighty chancy. I'm reckonin' on yore help, Eady.'

'Yu got it,' was the short reply. 'Fire away.'

'It means I got to trust yu, too, Quincy,' Sudden said to the scarfaced man. 'I don't know if I can.'

'Why, Sudden, what a thing to say!' exclaimed Shiloh, in mock tones of hurt feelings.

Green made no reply to this, but began to outline the idea he had had while skulking near the Apache camp. The Chiricahuas had lost a large number of their warriors during the fighting, and they were depressed and getting greedily drunk. The Apaches, he went on, abhorred night fighting not because it hampered them in any way but simply because they believed that the darkness was filled with the wandering spirits of their dead, and that these spirits would be displeased at anyone who disturbed their peace.

'I'm guessing that if we provided 'em with a few 'ghosts' it might just stampede 'em long enough for us to get out o' here an' make a run for it.'

'She's a mighty long shot, boy,' the old prospector told him.

'I know it,' was the quiet reply. '' Bout the on'y one we got, all the same.'

'S'posin' yore idea works, Jim,' Rusty interposed. 'Won't they still come after us when they catch on we've slid out?'

Sudden nodded. 'Shore they will. Which is why I'm suggestin' that instead o' headin' direct down the valley for Tucson we head straight into the desert, goin' south.'

'The desert? Yu want us to cross the desert?' squalled Shiloh Platt. 'What the hell for?'

''Cause it's about the last thing they'll be expectin' us to do,' Sudden told him. 'If we can build up a lead, we can get close to Fort Cochise afore they ketch up, an' mebbe they'll veer off on account o' the military patrols.'

'They's a lot of "ifs" in thar, Jim,' Eady remarked.

'That's sartin shore,' grinned the Texan. 'Danged near as many as there is if we stay here.'

'I don't fancy crossin' the desert in summer none a-tall, I'm tellin' yu,' grumbled Quincy. 'It gets mighty hot out there.'

'Hit gits hot in Hades, too, Quincy!' rapped old Eady, 'an' that's whar yu'll wind up sartin if yu set here an' wait for a merrycle.'

'Yu can take yore pick,' Sudden informed him coldly. 'Stay here an' be Injun-bait, or run the way they'll expect you to run. Either way yu'll lose yore precious hair.'

'How yu reckonin' on us gettin' clear, Jim?' Rusty asked, silencing the squabble.

'When them warwhoops see me 'n Eady, there oughta be some hootin' an' hollerin' goin' on,' the Texan said. 'Yu'll hear it clear. The minnit yu do, scratch dirt away from here. Ride due south. We'll ketch yu later, so don't go blazin' away at us when we come a-runnin' – jest in case yu got any ideas along them lines, Shiloh,' he said coldly, 'remember that the sound o' the shots'll carry plenty far in the night, an' Apaches has purty sharp ears.'

He returned his attention to Rusty. 'Load up some food, all the water yu can carry. Be ready to go the minnit yu hear yellin'.' He paused for a moment, to regard them all soberly. 'If yu hear shootin', however – sit tight. Any shots fired'll mean our li'l dodge came unstuck, an' we been took. Yu'll have to do the best yu can for yoreselves: Eady'n me won't be interested – much.'

This cool acceptance of the possibility of his own death at the hands of the bloodthirsty Apaches wrung an expression of admiration from even the slow-thinking Tucson.

'Yu'd do that – fer us?' he queried.

'On'y chance there is, Tucson,' was the smiling reply. 'I ain't plannin' on gettin' rubbed out unless it's – unavoidable.' His face went serious as he spoke again to Rusty. 'I'm relyin' on yu to look after the young lady,' he reminded Rusty. Rusty had absolutely no doubt what this tall drawling man who so composedly contemplated a grisly death meant, and he nodded. 'Don't yu fret none, Jim,' he told the older man. 'She'll be safe with me.'

A bold stare into Shiloh's face followed these brave words, and the half-breed's face darkened.

'Never doubted it for a minnit,' Sudden told him. 'Quincy, here's where I got to trust yu. If we pull 'er off, we'll be comin' back fast an' anxious to leave. We don't wanta waste time lookin' for hosses what ain't there – yu *sabe*?'

Quincy nodded. 'I sabe,' he leered. 'Yu reckon yu can trust me, Sudden?'

Tucson frowned and stepped in front of Quincy.

'Hell, Quince, yu wouldn't set a man afoot in Apache country when he's jest risked his life fer you, would yu?'

Quincy's face was a picture of deviltry, for he was enjoying this moment of power. It was pure mischief, but Shiloh's words put it on a totally different level.

'He might,' the half-breed hissed. 'Anyone here think he could stop him?'

That put Quincy's pride on the block; Shiloh Platt congratulated himself upon a particularly clever stroke. There would be little difficulty in cutting loose the horses of the two men before the party left, thus abandoning them and leaving the way clear for him to collect the reward money for the girl and keep it all for himself, for this was Shiloh's sworn intent. He found himself again set off-balance by the cold voice of Rusty.

'I'd stop him,' the boy said quietly.

Quincy lumbered to his feet, an evil grin on his lips.

'Yu reckon yu could take me – an' Shiloh?' he leered.

'I could try.'

Shiloh laughed harshly, but at the same moment, Tucson stepped in. 'Yu try anythin' like that, Quince, an' I'll back the kid's play,' the giant rumbled. His words tore away the last of Quincy's restraint. 'Yu big dumb oaf!' he screeched, and leaped for Tucson. The giant did not move; his huge ham-like fist swept around, catching Quincy on the point of his jaw, felling the scarfaced man like a slaughtered steer. Rubbing his knuckles, Tucson looked at the half-breed. 'Shiloh?' he said.

The half-breed backed away, his hands in front of him. 'No – now, take it easy, Tucson, I – I ain't. . . .'

'Got no guts?' Tucson gritted. 'Hell, that's plain. Yu goad Quincy into a corner, an' then when the chips go down, yo're missin'. What kind o' animal are yu, anyway, Shiloh?'

Shiloh looked around; he saw nothing but distaste on the watching faces. He turned to the girl, who stood nearest to him.

'Lissen,' he panted. 'Tell him. I didn't mean nothin' – it was a joke. I never reckoned Quince'd take it serious. Yu don't figger I'd leave a man afoot with them warhoops ready to take his hair, do yu?'

'I think that is exactly what you would do,' the girl said coldly. 'I also think you are a liar, a cheat, and a murderer.' These biting words were too much for Platt's control and rage flooded the flat, dark eyes. The Mexican blood had put a fierce and touchy pride in Shiloh's veins, and slighted, he reacted without thought of consequence.

'Why yu—' he spat, raising his arm to strike the cowering

girl. Before he could move it a foot higher, Sudden was across the room in one stride, and the barrel of a sixgun which had appeared magically in his right hand was jammed into Shiloh's middle.

'Go ahead, yu yeller dawg!' grated the Texan. 'An' I'll put yu down like the snake yu are!'

Shiloh Platt read death in Sudden's eyes, and his hand fell. He passed a hand across his eyes, to conceal the burning hatred in them, mumbling the while, 'Yu – look – I'm sorry. I didn't mean no harm. My temper—'

'Will get yu killed one o' these days,' snapped Sudden, stepping back and holstering the weapon in his hand. 'Get it under control – we got no more time to waste!'

Like a whipped cur, Shiloh Platt slunk away to one side and slouched into a chair, gazing vacantly at the wall, his mind a churning morass of seething hate.

'Yu'll pay,' he thought, the hate coursing through him like fire. 'All o' yu. And as for yu, my proud beauty, yu'll pay the highest o' them all. Afore I'm through with yu, yu'll beg on yore knees for a kind word from me.' With lurid pictures flickering in his twisted mind, Shiloh Platt hunched in his chair, ignoring the preparations of Eady and Sudden behind him. Presently the chastened Quincy joined him.

Night was closing in fast now, dropping like a curtain. It was black dark before long, with the diamond twinkle of stars in the velvet of the heavens, and a faint soughing wind which lifted tiny dust-devils, twirling them like faery dancers across the empty corral outside. Eady and Sudden worked quickly and efficiently.

From two grey saddle blankets they cut holes just large enough for their heads; when they tried them for fit, the blankets hung down almost to their knees. Nodding his satisfaction, Sudden poured some water on to the dirt floor, mixing up a small amount of greyish-black mud. This he proceeded to daub upon his face and hands, with Eady following suit. They both kicked off their boots, and stuck a sixgun each into their waistbands. Sudden laid his gunbelt aside with a meaning glance at Rusty, who sauntered idly over and stood close to the weapons.

'I'll see they're on yore saddlehorn,' he told Sudden. The puncher nodded and completed his preparations by donning the blanket and crouching slightly.

'How's she look, Tobias?' he asked.

'Purty gruesome,' Eady grinned through the mud on his face. 'I dunno what yu'll do to them 'paches, Jim, but yu shore as Gawd skeer the hell out o' me!'

A last-minute check to ensure that the arrangements were fully understood, and the two men eased out of the building. Snaking across the empty corral, they stopped in the deep shadow of the wall. The faint throbbing of a drum came from somewhere in the blackness.

'Scouts?' breathed Eady.

'None,' came the whispered reply. 'They ain't expectin' trouble.'

'Jes' as well,' hissed Eady. 'One wrong move an' the whole b'ilin's sp'iled.'

Sudden nodded. 'Let's go,' he muttered. His eyes gleamed faintly white in the darkness of his mud-smeared visage. Eady tried a practice flutter of the blanket enveloping him. In the darkness he looked like some huge, shapeless, grey-black thing, headless, armless, legless.

'Skeery enough?' he hissed.

'It better be,' was the sober reply. The two men slid now like shadows across the uneven ground, guided by the faint glow of the tiny Apache fires visible around a bend in the creek bed. Around the fires squatted the Apaches, chanting weirdly in time with the slow beating throb of a drum held by a *shaman*, or medicine man. When they were within thirty feet or so of the fires, Sudden touched the old man's arm, and signalled him to move off to the right. He himself edged left, matching Eady's progress so that their path forked to the sides of the Apache camp.

Moving now with infinite care, they came nearer to the glow of the fires. One cracking twig, one slithering stone, and they would be dead before they could get to their feet. Using every ounce of the skills taught him many years before by the old Piute horse-trader who had raised him, Sudden matched the crawling inch-by-inch progress of the old desert rat, whom he could see as a vague lump of darker blackness about ten feet or so to his right. The oldster was as well versed in this kind of work as any Indian; he had survived in these mountains only by knowing as many tricks as the Apaches, and one or two of his own as well. Sudden, counting to one hundred slowly beneath his breath, knew that Eady was doing the same. When he reached the end of his count, Sudden drew a deep breath, rose to his knees, and gave vent to as weird-sounding a moan as he could contrive. Eady appeared simultaneously from the ground a little distance away. The effect was electric.

The Apaches leaped to their feet, bug-eyed with fear and astonishment. For a moment that seemed as long as an aeon, they stood frozen, their weapons clutched in their hands. Then Eady moaned again, and added this time a gurgle so convincingly like a death-rattle that for a moment, the Texan's blood ran cold. It was the breaking-point. '*Ayeee!*' screamed one warrior. 'It is Death Face and his helper!'

Again Sudden moaned, and this time lurched forward, flapping the blanket. In the darkness he looked like some shapeless fiend. The Apaches broke. Like startled deer they scrambled for their horses or ran, their possessions forgotten, intent only upon outdistancing the terrible malevolent spirits behind them. Lashing their ponies madly they thundered out of the gully, fear lending wings to their headlong feet. The two men stood up in the boiling dust of their flight, Eady was laughing wheezily, slapping his thigh.

'I never seen the like,' he croaked, helplessly. 'Jim, yu shore beat all, the idees yu got!'

Sudden could not refrain from grinning. 'They musta thought their last hour'd come,' he agreed. 'Lady Luck shore smiled on us. Now let's fade afore they pluck up enough nerve to come back!'

Eady clapped his companion on the shoulder. Together the two men sped across the open ground to the station. There, tied to a viga pole, their horses stood, ready saddled.

'Good for yu, Rusty,' was Sudden's unspoken thought as he swung into the hurricane deck. He wheeled Nigger's head around, as Eady vaulted into his saddle with an agility that many a young man might have envied. They thundered out of the corral and down the slight declivity to the south where the faint dust raised by the fleeing defenders of Apache Wells hung glinting in the dark starlight. After about ten minutes' hard riding, they discerned the black bulk of the waiting quintet, who had heard their approach and were bayed ready with guns drawn.

'Hold it!' Sudden heard Rusty snap. 'It's Eady an' Green. Put yore guns up!'

Again the Texan thanked his stars for the hunch which had led him to juxtapose the youngster and Barbara Davis. Without Rusty there would have been every possibility that Quincy and Shiloh might have risked the chance of the Apaches hearing them, and shot him and the old man out of their saddles as they approached. They reined in alongside the waiting group.

'I reckon we razzle-dazzled 'em,' he panted. 'So we got mebbe an hour or two head-start.'

Rusty swung back into his saddle, saying: 'Let's make the most of 'er, then.'

'Hold on, thar!' The command came from old Eady, and they turned in surprise to face him.

'What's this?' whined Shiloh. 'We ain't got time—'

'Time a-plenty,' Eady said. 'Yu'll recall I told yu I wasn't ridin' along. This is whar our trails fork, gents.'

'Yo're takin' a mighty big chance alone, Tobias,' Sudden warned the oldster. 'It's yore skin, o' course, but—'

'But me no buts, Jim,' the old man grinned. 'I was doin' fine afore yu jaspers happened along an' brung yore 'pache frien's with yu. It's yu they's lookin' for, not a stringy ol' goat like me. I'm figgerin' I'll be a damn sight safer away from yu.'

Quincy spurred his horse forward. 'What d'yu mean, yu—'

'Yu heard me,' Eady snapped. 'I'm cuttin' loose. Yu boys foller yore own trail. I aim to go back to my prospectin', an' if yu don't like the idea, well—'

He swung his body to reveal the big old Sharp's rifle, cocked and levelled. Sudden frowned. The old man's attitude was contradictory, but after the endless years of shifting for himself, with only the rocks and his rifle for company, Eady was entitled to his decision.

'Sorry yu feel this way, Tobias,' he said. 'Ain't no point in tellin' yu I'd be glad to have yu backin' me this trip? Shore ain't no pleasure-jaunt we're facin'.'

'Like to oblige ye, Jim,' Eady said with regret, 'but scalp-huntin' ain't none o' my doin's. I'm lettin' yu go yore own way, an' I'm goin' mine. I suggest we get at it.'

'Aaaagh, stupid ol' goat!' snarled Shiloh Platt. 'Stay an' get yore ha'r lifted. Come on, we got to cover ground.'

Quincy hesitated for a moment, then wheeled his horse around. 'Yo're right,' he said. 'Let's ride, Sudden.'

Green nodded. 'Adios, ol' timer,' he said to Eady. 'Thanks for what yu done – back there.'

'No thanks needed,' Eady replied, his eyes meeting

Sudden's levelly. 'Even Steven, if yu ast me. We all got out with our ha'r on. *Adios,* Sudden. Watch yore back.'

'Bet on it,' Sudden said, and turned his horse to follow the party, which was moving already across the open ground, Quincy at its head, Shiloh and Tucson on the flanks, Rusty and Barbara Davis neatly hemmed in the middle. With a last wave to the old prospector, who sat watching them go, Sudden raced after the party. He was sorry to lose the backing of the old man, and felt somehow that there was something unexplained about Eady's withdrawal. He could not put a finger on what it was.

As he rode level with Tucson, the giant turned in the saddle to yell: 'Yu reckon we're clear, Green?'

'Hard to tell,' he said in reply. 'Apaches ain't fools – they'll ketch on soon enough to what we done. I'm just hopin' Juano won't think we're loco enough to go into the desert, an' mebbe follow a blind trail awhile afore he realizes we done just that.'

'Yu think it'll work?'

Sudden shrugged to indicate his uncertainty. Right now, the question of what the Apaches might or might not do was rapidly becoming a secondary consideration to the perils and problems of crossing the desert. But it was not far, and therefore just possible. If they could get across, high though the odds were against it, there was a chance that they could head down the San Pedrito valley to the umbrella shelter of Fort Cochise, where the presence of cavalry patrols might serve to keep the Apaches at their distance. This, in fact, was the basis of Sudden's gamble. 'Purty "iffy", all the same,' he told himself.

If Juano jumped to the conclusion that he hoped the Apache would; and if Shiloh and Quincy didn't bushwhack him before they reached safety. A wry grin touched his sombre face, and he recalled the long talk in Governor Bleke's office before he had set out upon this perilous mission.

Bleke had said at one point: 'Jim, if you don't make it—' and Sudden had interrupted him 'Shucks, seh, that li'l word "if" is shore a good jumpin' off place if a feller wants to give hisself grey hair. *If* I was a sensible *hombre,* I wouldn't be takin' this job on in the fust place. *If* I'm takin' it on, however, it ain't no use frettin' about what's goin' to happen *if* the Apaches try to trim my hair with a throwin' axe. *If* it happens, well – it happens. All the "iffin" in the world ain't goin' to alter it. So – *if* yu got any more o' that tobacco-juice yu call whisky, yu can give me a drink an' wish me luck. *If* yu don't mind!' The twinkle in his eye had drawn a broad smile from Bleke, and they had drunk a toast to Sudden's success.

'Which I'm hopin' yore luck's holdin', Governor,' Sudden muttered, peering ahead into the night as if trying to divine what lay beyond it.

CHAPTER ELEVEN

THE party pushed on through the night, and sunrise found them in a jumble of hills, surrounded on all sides by a desolate vista of cactus-dotted hogbacks, burning rocks and parched earth. Of this emptiness there seemed no end, but after another hour's riding the land levelled, and ahead of them appeared the shimmer, as if of water lying thin upon the ground, which indicated the proximity of the desert.

'That's it,' Sudden announced, pointing ahead. 'From here on it, it's nothin' but hot.'

The news was received in silence, each one's mind occupied with thoughts of the ordeal lying ahead. The sun climbed higher now above the blue darkness of the Dragoons, and its heat grew steadily stronger.

Presently Rusty pulled his horse alongside Sudden's and bent an inquiring gaze upon the tall Texan.

'Yu aimin' to cross the whole stretch, Jim?' he asked. 'She looks some wide.'

'Looks fool yu a mite,' Sudden replied, 'although at some points it's sixty, seventy miles across. This stretch o' desert ain't shaped reg'lar, however. She's kind o' U-shaped, an' I'm headin' for the bottom of the U, which ain't more 'n thirty miles across. After that there's some more country like this—' he made a gesture with his free hand,' – gullies an' hogbacks, good country to hide out in if we got to. But I'm hopin' it ain't goin' to be necessary. If them 'paches figger we took the easy road for Tucson, we might be able to get across afore they can catch up with us. Once we get in the vicinity o' Fort Cochise, they won't be too eager to start no shootin' match, in case the so'jer boys come out to see what's goin' on.'

'Good thinkin',' the younger man said. 'I'm on'y a mite worried about Quincy – he shore ain't goin' to be mad keen about ridin' into Fort Cochise.'

'I guess not,' was the reply. 'He ain't fool enough to think he's got much choice, however, an' that oughta clinch it.'

They rode in silence for a while, then Rusty spoke again. 'I got to thinkin' about what might happen to Bar – Miss Davis if anythin' went wrong with yore plan, Jim,' he said hesitantly. 'It could shore go hard with her.'

'Shucks, I'm set on avoidin' trouble,' Sudden told him. 'I ain't about to set Quincy an' Shiloh on the warpath on account o' nothin'. I don't want the reward money – that ain't my reason for mixin' in this shindig.'

'Why don't yu jest tell them that?' burst out the boy in astonishment, then, seeing the bleak look on his companion's face, he nodded. 'O' course, they wouldn't believe it, yu bein' Sudden.'

'That's right,' the Texan said, and his voice was harsh. Rusty looked up quickly at the tone in Sudden's voice, and then spoke softly.

'I never believed all I heard about Sudden,' he said. 'Yu don't look the owlhoot breed, Jim.'

Sudden smiled, the warmth lighting up his entire face and making him look strangely boyish for a moment.

'Which I'm thankin' yu, Rusty,' he said. 'Mebbe yu'd better hear the whole story. It might just be useful to yu in case yu ever get the easy money itch.' His voice was once more cold and hard, and as they rode along, the younger man listened in silence to the tale the black haired rider told, a tale of a promise to a dying man, and the blind search for two killers which had ensued. Sudden told Rusty how he had gained his reputation and his sobriquet, and of the false charge of murder which had sent him alone into the west, a price on his head, fair game for any man willing to try shooting him down.* At the end of the story, Rusty shook his head.

'What I said afore goes double, now, Jim,' he promised. 'I'll back yu any way I can. These jaspers'll try to cut yu out if they's any chance they can do it.'

'I imagine that li'l thought's been goin' around in Shiloh's noddle,' agreed Sudden. 'I'll just have to do my best to talk him out of it.' The frosty smile on his lips brought an answering grin to Rusty's face. The boy's eyes dropped for a moment to the smooth and deadly butts of the tied-down six-guns in their polished holsters. They shone dully in the faint starlight.

'If anyone can do it,' Rusty thought, 'yo're the one, Jim. I'm bettin' yo're square, an' I'm playin' it accordin'.' Thus committed in his own mind, he let his horse slow until he was once more alongside Barbara's. She smiled as he turned to tell her what he had just heard.

* * *

Shiloh, too was talking guardedly to Quincy, with Tucson riding nearby listening. A plan of dastardly dimensions was forming in Shiloh Platt's brain, and it contained all the ingredients for the revenge his slighted pride cried out for. He had begun planning the moment Sudden had mentioned his intention of heading for Cochise. Shiloh had no intention of going anywhere near the military, who wished to discuss with him certain dealings with reservation Indians which had resulted in Shiloh Platt receiving gold, and the hapless Pimas tobacco-coloured water which he had told them was whisky. Quincy, he knew could hardly dare show his face on a military establishment ... his mind busily wove a spiderweb of murder and deceit, discarding this eventuality, considering that.

'Once we get clear o' the desert we're sunk,' he told his companions. 'Mister Sudden aims to run for Fort Cochise, knowin' we can't show our faces there. That bein' the case

* **Related in SUDDEN – OUTLAWED (Corgi Books)**

he figgers to swindle us out o' the reward money, an' hightail it afore we can ketch up with him. Well,' he snarled, 'I ain't lettin' him.'

'How yu aimin' to stop him, Shiloh?' Quincy asked.

'I got an idea, don't yu worry,' the half-breed hissed. He glanced over his shoulder. Tucson had fallen back out of earshot. 'We get rid o' that stupid ox at the same time,' he gloated. 'I'll teach him to interfere in what don't concern him.'

'So,' breathed Quincy. 'We get rid o' Sudden an' Tucson. What then?'

'We change our route,' Shiloh told him with a cunning grin. 'Swing west, head across the desert an' come out right above—'

'Wilderness!' exclaimed Quincy. 'My Gawd, o' course!' He smiled, silently evil in the darkness. 'Shiloh, yo're a genius. Wilderness, o' course! No sheriff, no law, no interference. We hole up thar in peace until the ol' fool coughs up the mazuma, an' we're safe as ticks in a saddle-blanket.'

Shiloh nodded. The town of Wilderness was about twenty miles due north of Tucson; it had become the gathering-place for every scalphunter, owlhoot, desperado and murderer in the south-west. Any man who dared not show his face in Tucson gravitated to Wilderness, where there was no law, either Federal or Territorial. The outlaws policed the tiny mountain town themselves, and any man who entered it knew well that the penalty of jeopardizing the immunity of Wilderness was death. The retribution which the lawless visit upon their wayward own is far harsher than any other.

'Once we get there,' Shiloh said. 'We send word to the Davis gal's father, an' sit an' wait, like yu said, snug as bugs in a bedroll.'

'What about the kid?' Quincy wanted to know.

'Bah, he's sweet on the girl hisself,' Shiloh sneered. 'We

can use him for a messenger boy – if he gets to Wilderness alive.' The emphasis upon the last words was deadly and intent; case-hardened to violence though he was, Quincy shuddered at the cold-blooded manner in which his companion spoke of killing the boy.

'Takin' Green ain't goin' to be easy,' he warned Shiloh. 'He's too damn fast with them guns o' his!'

'Exackly,' said Shiloh with an evil smile. 'So we take him without guns. Then we'll see how long Mister Sudden lasts!'

'How yu figgerin' to do that?'

'I ain't,' was Shiloh's reply. 'Tucson is.'

'Tucson?' Quincy frowned in bewilderment. 'He backed Sudden afore. How—'

'Tucson'll do it,' Shiloh assured him. 'Yu leave everythin' to me.'

And with this dark promise, Quincy had to be content. He let his horse fall back, and Shiloh rode on alone, his mind tortuously following the possibilities of his loose-knit plan. Whichever way things worked out, one thing he knew for certain: at the end of it, the girl would be his. His mongrel blood thirsted for her cool beauty, and he seethed to have her in his power, begging for mercy, for a kind word. He would take her, break her; only then he would return her to her father.

* * *

They made camp that night in a declivity deep in the heart of the badlands, about half a mile from the edge of the desert itself. The sun had been strong throughout the day, and the rocks still retained its warmth these many hours later. On the morrow, they would head into the burning heart of the desert itself. Against the day, Sudden rationed the water stringently, as Shiloh had expected and hoped he would. When the cold food was prepared – they could not risk a fire – he passed Tucson his plate and in the darkness sprinkled it liberally with salt he had scraped up from a salt lick they had passed during their ride. The meat itself was heavily salted. By morning, the big man would have a monstrous thirst. Shiloh Platt rolled into his blankets with a satisfied grin on his lupine face.

They were awake before sun-up, having slept only a few hours. Once again, Shiloh made a point of grumbling about the rationing of the water.

'If we aim to get across that desert at all, we gotta save every drop o' water,' Sudden told him. 'The hosses'll need more 'n we will: yu know it as well as I do, so don't act up!'

'Hell, we ain't that short,' Quincy complained, acting upon Shiloh's nodded cue. 'Yu could give us another cupful at least.'

'No more water, an' that's final.'

'It's all right for yu, Sudden,' Shiloh sneered. 'What about pore Tucson here? He's a big feller. He needs more water 'n us others.'

'Got a Gawd-awful thirst on me fer shore,' Tucson admitted.

'Sorry, Tucson,' Sudden said with a shake of the head. 'Yu get the same as everyone else.'

'Ah, give the pore ox a break, Sudden,' wheedled Quincy. 'Go on, Tucson, get yoreself another swig o' water.'

'Shore could use another drink,' Tucson mumbled, half rising.

'Don't yu try it, Tucson!' Sudden's voice had gone cold and menacing, but Tucson lumbered to his feet.

'Shucks, Green,' he protested. 'One more cupful ain't goin' to make that much difference—'

'Go on, go on!' Shiloh rawhided the giant 'Yu ain't afeared o' him, are yu?'

Tucson shook his head, his dry tongue rasping across his lips. He wanted a drink. The idea was firmly in his head now. He had to have it. Shiloh was right. He was a bigger man than most: he needed more liquid. This thirst was torturing him. What right had Green to stop him, anyway?

'I ain't afeared o' nobody,' Tucson rumbled.

'Tucson!' Sudden's guns were in his hands in one smooth, eye-baffling movement, levelled rock-steady at the giant's barrel chest. Then Quincy's laugh broke the swift silence.

'Get yore water, Tucson,' he told the big man. 'If'n Sudden thar pulls trigger, every 'pache back within forty miles'll kill his pony gettin' here.'

Tucson looked at Sudden again, and took a step forward.

'I don't wanna hurt yu, Green,' he said.

'What I said still goes, Tucson,' Sudden told him quietly. 'Stay back.'

'I got to get me some water, Green!' burst out Tucson. 'I gotta.'

'No dice, Tucson. Yu got to move me first'

'Yu better get out o' my way,' Tucson said doggedly.

Sudden was puzzled by the man's persistence. Tucson was not a quick thinker, but only last night he had shown signs of understanding fair play as well as any man. Now – it just didn't make sense. The conviction deepened in his mind that Shiloh Platt had engineered this confrontation, but just how he could not now establish. The half-breed's goading had pushed Tucson to this point, and now the idea was firmly fixed in the huge man's brain to the exclusion of all else. The only way to stop Tucson was barehanded; he saw now that the man was conspicuously unarmed, and anyway, the scalphunters had been correct when they said that shooting would give away their position to the Apaches as surely as if they had lit a smoke fire to guide them. But stopping Tucson was going to be no easy task. Sudden's eyes weighed the barrel chest, the mighty shoulders and forearms, the height a good six inches above his own more than six feet.

Seeing Sudden's assessing glance, Shiloh Platt jeered,

'Don't make the mistake o' tryin' to stop him, Sudden – he'd break yu in two!'

Rusty stepped forward, standing alongside his friend, hand curled above his gun butt. Sudden waved him back.

'No gunplay,' he told the boy. 'It's too dangerous.'

'Then let him have the water!' urged Rusty. 'It ain't that important.'

'It ain't the water we're arguin' over,' Sudden said. 'It's on'y a means to an end. Shiloh figgers that if Tucson breaks a few o' my bones, then I'll hardly be able to stop him callin' the tune from here on in.'

'Let him call it,' the boy said. 'What's the odds – we'll still get Barbara home.'

'I ain't so shore o' that,' was the reply, and a quick glance at Shiloh revealed a start of surprise at Sudden's words. The Texan knew now that his hunch was right, and that Shiloh had somehow engineered the affair.

'Tucson,' he said calmly. 'Yu know yo're bein' used, don't yu?'

Tucson shook his head. 'All I know is I'm dyin' o' thirst while yore a-jabberin', Sudden. Whyn't yu step aside an' let me get my drink o' water?'

Sudden raised a hand in the halt sign, his mind made up.

'Hold it right there, Tucson!' he snapped. The giant halted, a frown between his beetling brows. Sudden beckoned with his forefinger, and Tucson leaned forward; what was the man playing at, anyway? In a second he knew.

Starting almost level with his ankles, Sudden's right fist came flashing upwards in a murderous uppercut, every ounce of his whipcord strength behind it. His fist caught Tucson flush on the point of the jaw, and sent him flailing backwards to land with a crash upon the ground, a cloud of dust fogging up around him. Sudden watched him, eyes narrowed. Tucson lay still for a moment, eyes closed; and Sudden began to hope that perhaps his desperate gamble had paid off. Then Tucson moved. He rose on one elbow, then got to his knees, rubbing the dust-matted blood from his split lips. He looked up at Sudden with a dull light that grew brighter in his eyes, and a slow smile began to spread across his face. And then Sudden knew that he was in for a fight.

The big man came at him like a bull, and Sudden evaded the huge hands, skipping away and chopping down with his right fist on the back of Tucson's neck as he did so. His only hope, he knew, was to keep out of the man's clutches. Those ham-like hands and tremendous arms would break him like a dry stick if they ever closed about him. Time after time, he dodged Tucson's ungainly rushes, punishing the big man with flurries of punches to the face, aiming for Tucson's beetling brows, cutting them, half blinding him with blood. Every time Tucson reached up to paw the streaming blood from his eyes, Sudden would move in and out fast, planting solid vicious blows to the midriff, one-two, one-two, putting every ounce of power he could muster behind them. For all the outward difference it seemed to make he might as well not have tried, for Tucson shrugged off the punishment and kept coming after Sudden, growling inarticulately, his splayed hands reaching, pawing. Once or twice he landed glancing blows which sent Sudden reeling, his mind jarred by the sheer power of those huge fists, but the Texan managed to remain on his feet. He knew with deathly certainty that if he fell, Tucson would show no mercy, for the giant was now mindlessly fighting without thought of cause or effect, fighting because that was what he did superbly, the huge strength channelled into its perfect outlet.

Lumbering, clumsy, unstoppable, he pursued the will-o-the-wisp Texan, who danced away from his reach like a wraith. Once, he caught Sudden's shirt in a huge paw, and a yell of triumph escaped him, only to end in an oath of chagrin as Sudden wrenched free, leaving a square of ripped cotton in the man's grasp, and then slashed two punishing blows into Tucson's ribs. The blood was pouring down the giant's face, and he brushed it away with an oath of rage. Again, Sudden hit him hard in the midriff, solid blows that pushed a gasp from the giant's puffed lips. The big head dropped for a moment, and once more Sudden drove it up with a full-blooded uppercut. Tucson rocked on his heels, stunned for a moment, and then shook his head. Sudden stood back, his chest heaving, fists still cocked and ready. Would nothing even slow down this bearlike figure? Again, Tucson rushed forward, and again Sudden, fists clubbed, chopped savagely at the man's exposed neck. Tucson stumbled to one knee, but this time instead of stopping there for a moment he whirled, and tossed a fist almost casually sideways. It caught Sudden with all his weight on one foot as he moved sideways; only a glancing blow in the ribs, but enough to wind him and send him reeling back against a boulder. Moving with astonishing speed for one so huge, Tucson whirled around and the huge forearms wrapped themselves around the puncher's body, as vicious and irresistible as a metal vice, squeezing the breath from his lungs, torturing his rib cage. Red spots, then black swamped the Texan's vision, and he knew unconsciousness was very near. With a roar of triumph, Tucson leaned back, lifting, taking Sudden's feet off the ground so that his entire weight was gripped in the crushing circle of Tucson's arms. With a superhuman effort, Sudden doubled his legs behind him, thrusting with the soles of his feet against the boulder. This unexpected move pushed Tucson backwards, slightly off balance, and for a moment the crushing strain of his grip was relaxed, and in that moment, Sudden, his arms spread and his palms open, smashed both hands simultaneously against the giant's ears. Tucson screamed in agony, and his hands went to his ears, for the terrible blow Sudden had given him had felt like a steam hammer exploding inside his skull. Sudden reeled clear, wheezing for oxygen, his tortured lungs labouring to return to normal. Sweat drenched him, and his arms felt as if leaden weights were attached to them. Tucson was standing, reeling slightly, shaking his head. His face showed the results of the murderous punches that Sudden had landed upon it. Tucson's lips were split and puffed, his eyebrows matted with dried blood, a huge darkening bruise on one cheekbone. Now Sudden moved in for a final try: while Tucson was still half-dazed from the effects of that awful impact upon his ears, The Texan delivered one, two, three, four sledgehammer punches to Tucson's middle. The giant's breath hissed out of his lungs and he wilted, but even under this merciless hail of blows, he slouched forward, arms reaching blindly for the man in front of him. Sudden edged backwards, this time quite close to where Quincy and Shiloh stood, and realized his danger too late. Although he half-turned to avoid the peril, he was unable to avoid the push from the scalphunter which sent him reeling forward on one knee directly in front of the oncoming Tucson.

'There y'are, yu dumb ox,' yelled Quincy. 'Finish it!'

With a tremendous roar of mingled rage and triumph, Tucson swung a haymaker at the stumbling form he could just see through the blood which misted his eyes. The blow caught Sudden on the side of the head and lifted him bodily two or three feet to be hurled in a crumpled heap against the boulders ringing the edge of the campsite. Tucson stood in the centre of the clearing, his shoulders heaving, and looked at the body of his fallen adversary. He shook his head.

'Yu needn't of shoved him,' he complained. 'I would've taken 'im!'

Barbara Davis knelt quickly over the unconscious Sudden as Quincy raged 'Yu big dumb ox, he was runnin' yu ragged! If I hadn't shoved him in front o' yu, he'd've cut yu down like the slow hunk o' choppin' meat yu are!'

He made to turn away, but Tucson, frowning now, pulled him back with a ham-like hand which took a fistful of the scarfaced man's shirt and half-lifted him off his feet.

'Why's it matter to yu whether I beat him?' he roared. 'What difference does it make to yu, Quincy?'

Quincy wrenched ineffectively against the big man's grip as Shiloh plucked tentatively at Tucson's arm. Quincy's face darkened, and then the scar across his face went a livid white. His eyes began to roll in his head.

'Put me down, yu dolt!' he bellowed. 'Let – go o' me!'

Tucson's homely face creased into a frown beneath its mask of dust and blood. He shook Quincy like a terrier shaking a rat. 'That's another thing,' he raged. 'Don't yu keep callin' me stupid. Yu hear me?' He shook Quincy. 'Don't call me that.'

'Dolt! Ox!' Flecks of foam appeared at the corners of Quincy's mouth as the others watched helplessly while Tucson shook the bearded scalphunter like a rag doll. 'Let – go – Tucson!' screamed Shiloh, dancing around. 'Yu ape, let him go!'

The half-breed's words touched Tucson's consciousness, and he lashed out with his free hand, sending Shiloh reeling back, blood pouring from his pulped lip. As he did so, his grip on Quincy loosened slightly, and the scarfaced scalphunter, the bright light of madness in his eyes, squirmed his body around and with his free hand whipped out his revolver. Thrusting the muzzle against Tucson's chest he pulled the trigger. The report was muffled, and Tucson doubled up like a jack-knife, reeling backwards, his shirt burning where the powder-flash had ignited it. Tucson painfully drew himself upright and lurched forward, hands outstretched for Quincy, then fell to the ground in a boneless heap as a thin scream escaped Barbara Davis's lips.

Quincy's mad gaze swept the others. He was raging with

passion, his whole body – save only the hand which held the smoking sixgun – trembled with it. He had killed and he hungered to kill again. Even Shiloh, inured to violence as he was, shrank back, awed by an anger such as he had rarely witnessed. All of them knew that a word, a slight movement might turn the camp into a shambles. In his blind insensate fury Quincy would shoot and go on shooting until nothing stood except himself.

'Who's next?' he barked. 'Who else wants to argue?' His baleful, bloodshot eyes travelled to Rusty, who knelt beside the still form of Sudden.

'Yu, kid?' grated Quincy. 'Yu got anythin' to say? Step out an' pull yore gun an' we'll settle this right now!'

'Quince . . .' Shiloh Platt ventured.

'Shut yore mouth, damn yu!' hissed Quincy. 'This is my shindig an' yu'll do what I'm tellin' yu to do.'

'Yu reckon the Apaches will as well?' Rusty looked up from where he knelt, and his cool question made Quincy stop, a puzzled look on his face. He shook his head as if to clear it, and those watching saw the killing light begin to dim in his eyes.

'Yu've blown it now, Quincy,' Rusty went on inexorably. 'That shot'll bring every 'pache buck within twenty miles o' here at a dead run.'

Quincy's shoulders slumped, and his face seemed to grow older. He passed a hand wearily across his eyes, then looked at Shiloh Platt. The half-breed saw that the madness was gone, and at the same time realized his opportunity. He stepped forward with his own gun drawn.

'Shuck yore gunbelt, Rusty!' he snapped. '*Move!*'

For a moment, it looked as if Rusty might argue the point, but at that moment Barbara Davis, fearing further bloodshed, touched his arm. With a sigh, Rusty unbuckled his belt and stood away from his weapons. Shiloh scooped them up and tossed them across his saddle.

'Yu show good sense, girlie,' Shiloh grated. 'Quince, get me some rope.'

'I don't get this, Platt,' Rusty said, frowning.

'Yu will,' promised the half-breed. 'Quince, tie that black-haired sonofabitch good. If the Apaches is on their way here like the kid sez, they're goin' to find somethin' to keep their minds off of us long enough to give us time to get clear.'

Rusty watched in astonishment as Shiloh revealed his monstrous intent, the enormity of the foul deed beyond his understanding. 'For Gawd's sake, Platt!' he cried. 'Yu can't leave him here for the Injuns!'

Shiloh Platt cocked the sixgun and pointed it at Barbara Davis. 'Yu want to bet her life on it, sonny?' he snapped. When Rusty turned away, disgust on his face, Shiloh grinned mirthlessly. 'I thought not. Mount up: let's get the hell outa here afore them red sons arrive! His gaze raked the small clearing, passing over the still forms of Tucson and the unconscious Texan.

'I hope they roast yu alive, Sudden,' he gloated. 'One thing's shore: yu won't bother me no more!'

Quincy led his horse over. 'Green's nag bolted,' he reported. 'Damn brute near took my hand off when I tried to get close.'

'Leave it,' Shiloh snapped. 'Mister Sudden ain't goin' to be needin' it!'

Without another word he spurred his horse out of the clearing, Rusty and Barbara riding behind him, Quincy bringing up the rear. The dust of their going had not yet settled when Sudden groaned and opened his eyes.

CHAPTER TWELVE

HIGH in the molten sky a tiny speck wheeled. Slowly it came nearer, dropping slightly, tilting its wings to catch the faint thin breeze that touched the tips of the faraway mountains. It swooped lower; then hovered. A triumphant croak came from its throat: the buzzard had sighted prey. Gliding slowly downwards towards the tumbled rocks, always wary for movement – for the buzzard is a coward who prefers to feast upon the maimed or the dead – the ugly black bird settled, with a flapping of its heavy wings, upon a boulder above the clearing where Sudden lay motionless.

Sudden had watched the bird land, however; and a curse escaped his lips.

'Hell,' he muttered. 'I'd better give that brute some sign I'm alive, or he'll be down here peckin' my eyes out afore yu can holler "grub-pile".' He surged against the bonds which held him, struggling violently; but Shiloh Platt had done his job well, and the bonds gave not an inch. The sweat glistened on the Texan's brow as he strained every muscle against the restricting ropes, and then subsided with a gasp. It was no use. A quick glance showed that the malevolent bird had hopped down to a nearer stone, its wicked eyes glinting in the sun. Up in the sky two circling dots signalled the advent of more of its kind. Then, without warning, the big black bird gave a startled squawk and leaped into the air, climbing fast and high away from the rocks. Sudden watched it go with a frown touching his brows, an expression which quickly changed to one of foreboding. 'Somethin' movin' out there in the rocks,' he reasoned, half-aloud. 'An' whatever it is, it shore ain't help a-comin'.' Nor was it. In a few more moments, as if rising from the very rocks themselves, two Apache warriors appeared. They approached cautiously, their short bows strung with iron-tipped arrows which Sudden knew would be coated with deadly venom. One of the warriors sidled over to Tucson's body, turning it over and kicking it violently. To Sudden's amazement, he heard a groan of pain. Then Tucson was still alive! He had not time to carry the thought further, for the second warrior stood over him now, his reptilian eyes burning with dark hatred. Levelling the nocked arrow full at the helpless Texan's chest, the Apache drew back the bowstring slowly, to its fullest extent.

'Stop!'

The voice was familiar, and Sudden twisted his head to see its owner, Juano, step out from behind the rocks and stride forward, his eyes blazing with triumph. Sudden felt almost glad to see the big Apache. That warrior's bowstring had been about an inch from the point of release, and although Sudden had looked death many times in the face, he could not repress a shudder.

To poison their arrows, the Apaches taunted rattlesnakes until the reptiles disgorged their venom. They used this, mixed with other deadly ingredients, as a mixture to dip their war arrows into. The slow convulsions which the merest scratch from such an arrow brought on, and the lingering death which followed, were not Sudden's idea of the way he would have chosen to die. To go down fighting against superior odds, to have at least a chance – a man could ask no more. But poison . . . again, in the hot sunlight, a shiver touched his body. None of these feelings showed on his face, however. He turned his head to face the Apache leader.

'Long time no see,' he managed, casually.

The Apache stepped forward and towered over the bound prisoner, his painted visage contorted with cruelty.

'Soon you no laugh!' he spat.

'Oh, I dunno,' Sudden said. 'Allus try to see the funny side o' things, that's my motto. Seen any ghosts lately?'

The remark brought the blood rushing into the Apache's face, and the veins stood out like cords upon the copper forehead. For a chilling moment, Sudden thought he had gone too far, but Juano controlled himself with an effort.

'You trick Apache twice,' he ground out. 'Not third time!' A curt command and Sudden was dragged to his feet, and he was cut loose long enough to mount a pony. As soon as he was on the animal's back, his feet were roped beneath its belly. He watched as two warriors struggled to slide the huge body of Tucson face down across the back of a horse, where his dangling arms and feet were roughly lashed to prevent his body sliding off. Sudden ventured a question, and the Apache sneered.

'Big man not dead,' he told the Texan. 'Maybe wish he was, soon.'

The horses were brought and on a command from the leader, they set off at a lope into the desert ahead. Sudden counted the band: seven warriors and Juano. No sign of Manolito. It was possible that the war party had been split up, with Manolito and the rest of the warriors following the valley trail in case the pursued party had gone that way. The Texan noted too that several of Juano's warriors had no ponies. They seemed unworried by this, nor did their fellows appear to find it remarkable. They kept up effortlessly with the jogging ponies, moving in an economical ground-eating dog trot. Sudden recalled the stories he had heard of Apache warriors, who could run fifty miles in a day and fight a battle at the end of it. They were men of iron constitution and indomitable will; and they would fight the white man until they were all killed or their spirits were broken. Sudden was not one of those who held the cynical view that the only good Indian was a dead one. Cochise and Mangas Coloradas, Red Cloud, Tecumseh, Dull Knife, these had been great men no matter what the colour of their skin. White men never stopped to consider that it was they who were the interlopers, and that the red man was being robbed and cheated on all sides simply never occurred to them. To most frontiersmen, the red man was a menace to life, and he treated the Indian as he would any other plague – by doing his best to wipe it off the face of the earth. Sudden wondered now how the others were faring. Had they managed to conceal their tracks? It had been a surprise to find these Chiricahuas so far west, and so deep into the desert; this was proof of Juano's determination to avenge himself upon the white-eyes who had so cleverly tricked him. Sudden stole a glance at the Apache leader. He rode with his head high, a tiny smile of satisfaction playing around the cruel mouth which boded ill for the prisoner.

Sudden shrugged; it was not in his nature to despair, and he managed to maintain an air of sardonic indifference to his fate, even though he realized this would only further anger his captors. Once, when an unlucky stumble flung a warrior against a cactus, he laughed with the others at the Apache's frenzied actions as he wrenched the wicked spikes from his flesh. Sudden's coolness surprised the watching warriors; in his predicament, their prisoners usually begged, screamed, blubbered for mercy.

Finally they came to a stop. They were in the middle of a wide flat stretch of open desert, bare of even cactus or mesquite, heavy rocks scattered here and there. Since it was still bright day, Sudden knew that this was not a camping place, but where he was to die. He looked at Juano as one of the warriors slashed through the bonds around his feet and dragged him roughly to the ground, and saw that he had guessed correctly; the Apache's face was like a stone carving of some evil, ancient god. When Juano spoke, there was a silken menace in his words.

'You understand? Juano want you die very slowly. You

die here where nothing live. No water, nothing That one—' he jerked a hand towards the figure of Tucson, lying now on the ground, '—maybe die quicker, bring black birds. No matter – you die very slow.'

'Shucks, yo're just mad 'cause yu made a poor trade,' Sudden retorted, unabashed by the Apache's icy words. 'By the way – yu shot any o' them Winchesters yet?'

This reminder of the trick which had shamed him before his warriors shattered the Indian's control and turned him into a raving beast. With eyes glazed and body shaken by rage, he rained blows upon the defenceless prisoner, who stood them unmoved, a contemptuous sneer on his lips. Juano snatched a knife from his belt and raised it, and then, just as suddenly as he had begun, stopped, a look of cunning seeping into the lizard eyes.

'Almost you trick Juano again,' he said, and thrust the wicked Bowie knife back into its sheath. 'But you no die so easy. You die Apache way: slowly. Your tongue burst in your mouth. Your body turn to fire. Your brain make you *maricon*.'

'I'll go crazy, all right, if yu keep on chatterin',' said the unmoved Texan. 'Yu got me so scared my knees is rattlin'.' If there was any truth in what he said, there was no evidence of it in his demeanour, which was upright and fearless.

'*Enju!* It is enough!' snapped Juano. Sudden's wrists were freed, and a strip of rawhide was lashed to each wrist, hanging loose. The same procedure was adopted for his ankles. While this was being done, another warrior, using a heavy flat stone, hammered four stakes into the ground making a rough approximation of a rectangle. A stunning blow from the butt of a rifle sent Sudden reeling to the stony ground, and the thongs at his wrists and feet were lashed in turn to the immovable stakes. He lay there, stretched in the tight X of his bonds, while the Indians repeated the procedure with the still-unconscious Tucson's body. A quick, unobserved testing of his bonds told Sudden that there was no play in them whatsoever.

Now the Apaches brought a water skin, and poured some on each of the thongs. Sudden's blood went chill; in the hot sun, the thongs would shrink rapidly, stretching his body as if on a rack. But Juano was not yet done. He now took a tiny sack, made from tanned and softened deerhide, from the cantle of his crosstree saddle and came over to the recumbent prisoner, Two of the warriors roughly ripped away the Texan's shirt, and Juano leaned forward, emptying the contents of the sack upon Sudden's chest. The puncher's eyes narrowed: honey! He arched his back and shook his head from side to side in an effort to avoid the sticky stream Juano poured on him, but to no avail: his efforts merely spread the sweet stuff more evenly about him. Juano poured it until the sack was empty and Green's chest, face, and the ground beneath his head were covered with the stuff. Juano stood back to survey his handiwork.

'Now we see if white-eye can think of trick to make desert ants stay away,' he snarled.

The Apache well knew that ere long the murderous red ants of the desert would come in hordes, attracted by the sweet smell of the honey, picking, biting, stinging Sudden in a torment of tiny pains until he went berserk, driven insane by the double torture of the racking rawhide and the merciless insects.

'He who would cheat Apache should remember: Apache have long memory,' Juano finished. 'Think upon that, white-eye.'

'Aw, yo're jest a sore loser,' Sudden said with a grin, although he felt far from in a grinning mood. The awful sentence of death which the Apache had pronounced upon him was in some ways less preferable than the fate he had earlier escaped.

Juano leaped on to the back of his horse, reining the animal's head cruelly around. 'Now we go: find your friends,' he said, with a snarling grin. 'Got plenty more honey.' And with this chilling threat, he signalled to the warriors, who began to troop away from this place of death. The prisoner watched them move up the side of a slight swell in the land, then vanish down the far side, moving south. He assessed his own position. It looked pretty hopeless. No horse, no weapons, no water, not even a sharp stone near his tight-drawn hands or feet to try to shuffle around towards the wet rawhide thongs. And even if he did get free, without his horse and guns, without water, getting out of the desert on foot was well-nigh impossible.

'Damnation!' he said aloud. 'I ain't licked yet!'

His voice sounded scratchy and dry in his throat, and he realized that the terrible heat of the desert was already leeching the moisture from his body. He knew he must act as fast as he could, while he still had his strength. The rawhide thongs would also dry out very quickly, and he must move before they did.

'Gawd, what I'd give for a drink!' he gasped.

Something tickled his ear, and he shook his head, then recoiled in horror. A rapid glance showed him several big red ants moving in their busy half circles around the pool of honey which had trickled from his face and body to the ground. Sudden knew that there was not a moment to lose. If those insects moved on to his defenceless skin, his face, his eyes . . . he repressed a shudder, with difficulty. The rawhide thongs were still darkly damp, and he arched his body, heaving with every ounce of his strength against the restraining stakes. The thongs bit viciously into his unprotected wrists, but he gritted his teeth, ignoring the searing pain, and arched his body again. Grinding his teeth, he surged against the restraining thongs until it seemed as if they must surely cut through his wrists like butter. He fell back, gasping. Had there been a slight movement? The thongs were still wet enough to stretch slightly, and if he could just pull them enough before the sun dried them, there was a faint chance . . .

'Ain't much o' one, but any's better'n none at all,' he managed, the sound of his voice hoarse and cracked now. He knew that he must hurry.

Again and again he arched his body, surging against the bonds, panting for breath in that ovenlike atmosphere, the heat beating down upon his perspiration-bathed body like a brazen hand, his throat tight and fiery. A searing pain burned his skin and he looked down. The ants had followed the trail of honey up his heaving body and were now moving across his bared chest in a dark clotted mass. Sudden ground his teeth to keep from crying out at the incessant pain of their infinitesmal bites, shaking his head violently to keep the insects from getting on to his face. Doggedly he kept working on the rawhide thongs, tensing and pulling, feeling them give a tiny fraction more each time, leaving now a small amount of play. But the terrific exertion and the relentless sun were taking their toll. Sudden looked up at the molten ball in the sky with dust-rimmed eyes, and croaked a weird curse. Once more he surged against his bonds, and this time he felt the first real movement. He tested the right hand thong and found that it had stretched perhaps two inches. The left hand one was also appreciably longer, certainly long enough to enable him to ease downwards on his back until he felt his heel touch the stake to which his right foot was bound. A sigh escaped his puffed lips. Now once more, with renewed vigour, he arched his back. Using his shoulders as a prop, he drove his right foot in a downward stabbing kick at the stake. The high heel of his boot jarred against the squat wooden peg, jolting the bound man's entire body; but now he was desperate, and the strength which drove him was the last remaining strength of sanity. Again the right foot stabbed out and again, and now the stake moved, and moved, and then in one last surging kick he knocked it out of the ground. Now he rolled up on his right knee, heaving until it was under his body, ignoring the nettling bites of the ants still guzzling their sticky feast. He threw all his weight backwards against the thong binding his left foot. Once, twice, three times he repeated this movement, then all at once the stake came out of the ground, and Sudden fell backwards, gasping for breath. Faint now, and racked with pain, longing for rest which he knew he dare not take, he lay for a moment until his breathing was as near normal as it would get in this furnace heat. Then slowly he got to his feet, his body doubled forward, and in a few more minutes had dragged the stakes which held his hands clear of the brittle earth. With his neckerchief he wiped off the gooey mess of honey and with it the torturing ants. His whole chest was a mass of tiny bites, red and angry; and his wrists were swollen to nearly twice their normal size, with deep red weals made by the rawhide. But these hurts were as nothing to the raging thirst which possessed him.

'Got . . . to . . . get water,' he croaked. 'Get . . . water.'

He staggered over to the side of the giant Tucson, who lay unconscious still, the front of his body covered in a sticky mess of dried blood. Struck by an inspiration, the Texan lifted the big man's head and felt down the back of Tucson's neck *Yes!* The hunch had paid off. Like many frontiersmen, Tucson had kept a hideaway knife in a sheath tucked down between his shoulderblades. Sudden slid the knife out and with weary strokes, cut the giant's hands and feet free. With bleary eyes, he surveyed the area. About a hundred and fifty yards away he saw the candlestick shape of a small saguaro, and he stumbled towards it, the knife dangling in his hand. Ignoring the wicked spikes, he slashed the stem of the cactus, and again, slicing a hunk perhaps six inches long away from the plant. Between the core and the spiny outer skin lay a central pulp which contained, if not water, at least moisture. His hands trembling with weakness, Sudden stripped away the thorny skin and then, crushing the pulp between his hands, he let the life-giving liquid drip like nectar into his parched throat. When he had exhausted the pulp, he cut another piece and repeated the process. Then he cut a third slice, and jamming the knife into it, tottered back towards the still form of Tucson.

'It ain't enough,' he muttered, his thirst still far from satisfied. 'But it's shore better than none at all.' Lifting the man's head, he squeezed a few drops of the liquid into Tucson's still-puffed lips. The giant groaned, and his eyelids flickered slightly. Sudden marvelled at the man's constitution. Any ordinary man who had been through half of what Tucson had suffered would have been dead long ago; yet still the giant lived.

He tore away the powder and blood-blackened shirt and his eyes narrowed as he saw the terrible wound, low down on Tucson's side. A quick examination showed no exit wound: the bullet was still inside Tucson. Sweat beaded the big man's brow for an instant, only to evaporate as soon as it formed. The bullet hole was surrounded by a huge purple swelling, veined and shiny. When he touched it, the unconscious man's breath hissed through his teeth.

'Easy, Tucson,' he said. He cleaned the wound as best he could, and with strips of Tucson's shirt and neckerchief made a pad and bandage, binding the wound roughly. 'It ain't much,' he apologized to the unconscious man. 'But about the best I c'n manage.' He shook his head; Tucson needed a doctor, medical aid. He glanced at the sinking sun. Night would bring a slight relief, but it would be accompanied by the chill of the desert night, and in Tucson's feverish state, the cold could well be fatal. He cursed his own helplessness. His body still screamed for water. He knew that if they did not soon find more, they would both die. In vain he shook his head; the visions of tumbling waterfalls, the clear and leaping mountain streams he had forded so many times, the slow and majestic rolling of the Gila and San Pedro persisted in his mind. His imagination was so vivid that as night came he held out a wondering hand, so real was the sensation of falling rain. He laughed harshly, and there was a touch of madness in the sound. As if hearing it, Tucson opened his eyes, trying weakly to sit up. His glance touched the hunched form of Sudden.

'Uh . . . Jim? Jim, is that . . . yu?' managed the big man. 'Where in – Hades are we?'

'Yu got it in one, Tucson,' croaked Sudden grimly. 'Hades is as good a name for it as any.'

Tucson struggled weakly to rise on one elbow, his hand moving instinctively to the bound wound in his middle. 'Jest lie easy,' Sudden told him. 'Yu ain't nowheres near fit enough to sit up.'

When Tucson asked again how they had come to be in this wilderness, Sudden explained briefly the events which had taken place while Tucson had been unconscious. He made a wry gesture at the two last hunks of the saguaro which he had brought to where they sat.

'That's all the water we got, Tucson,' he told the giant. 'It ain't enough to keep a Gila monster goin' for a day in this desert. We got to find more.'

'Wal . . . I ain't shore . . . as how I can travel, Jim,' Tucson gasped. 'Thisyere – tickles, some.' He smiled apologetically, and Sudden turned to him. 'Tucson, I'm a fool,' he swore. 'I'm too damn' busy thinkin' about my own skin.'

Tucson shook his head. 'Yu ain't that,' he managed. 'On'y I – reckon yu'd better – head on out – alone, Jim,' he smiled weakly. 'I'll jest – slow yu down.'

'I ain't so chipper my own self,' Sudden replied grimly. 'We better rest up tonight, an' see how things look in the mornin'. Mebbe we'll find a few more o' them saguaros.'

'Yeah ... mebbe,' agreed Tucson, rolling back, unconscious before his head touched the ground, his breath rasping through his swollen lips. Sudden gazed at the recumbent form, torn by the dilemma he faced. He was not strong enough to carry Tucson, and the big man could certainly never walk far. He could not abandon Tucson, and yet he knew that with every passing minute the danger to his own life, alone in the desert without water, increased tenfold. He scuffled around in the darkness and found some dry sticks. With these he fashioned a tiny fire, Apache fashion; somehow he must keep the biting night cold off the wounded Tucson. The fire glowing in the darkness, he lay down to try to snatch a few hours' rest, the problem still unresolved.

CHAPTER THIRTEEN

SUDDEN awoke.

It was still dark, with only the slightest faint streak of grey in the eastern sky to herald the approach of dawn. He lay for a moment, trying to define the reason for his own awakening, and then he knew he had heard a sound. Something alien had moved nearby and even in his exhausted sleep, the sixth sense of the frontiersman had transmitted a warning to his body. Without raising his head, Sudden swept the surrounding area with his eyes. Tucson lay on his back, unmoving; he could hear the big man's stertorous breathing. The tiny fire was almost dead; only an infinitesimal glow lingered beneath the pile of wood ash. Easing himself on to his side, moving with infinite caution, Sudden opened his eyes, closed them, opened them again and closed them, repeating this until he was properly accustomed to the half light. His arms and legs were stiff and sore; penalty, he knew, for the Herculean exertions of the preceding day. A faint slithering sound touched the edge of his hearing, and his hands moved instinctively to his hips. The empty holsters mocked the gesture.

The Apache came out of the bushes with a shrieking yell, and Sudden, twistling like an eel to avoid the diving downward thrust of the knife in the Indian's hand, shouted 'Tucson!' He saw the big man sit up and then wince, his hand going to his wound, as the Apache hit the ground scrambling on his knees. Sudden moved back now, his left hand reaching for the thrusting, glinting knife, his right pulling Tucson's hideaway weapon from his own belt. The Apache came in in one smooth sweeping run, and Sudden rolled backwards, taking the Indian down with him and pushing up and outwards with the knife, burying it to the hilt in the Apache's heart as the grease-slippery body hurtled over his own. He felt the wiry body tense as the steel bit deep and he pulled back, and was on his feet now, ignoring the dead warrior. Picking up the fallen knife that the Apache had held, he turned to see Tucson on his feet, roaring out oaths, two warriors clinging to him as he swung around like some great grizzly bear, both of them trying to free themselves long enough to strike at him with their knives. With a terrible oath, Tucson lifted one of them in his mighty arms and raised him high up above his head. Then he smashed the Indian to the ground. The warrior writhed once, his face contorted in agony, then lay still, his back broken. The other raised his knife hand to slay the giant Tucson, who had dropped to one knee, bright fresh blood staining the bandage where his wound had burst open. The fell blow was never delivered. In the same second Sudden hurled the heavy knife in his hand. It turned only once, winking in the faint traces of morning light, and buried itself in the Apache's throat. With a muted gurgle he melted to the ground. Tucson dropped to one knee, supporting himself on the flat of his right hand, coughing weakly. Sudden, with a quick glance around to make sure that no further Apaches skulked nearby, dashed over to the big man's side. Tucson had fallen, and was lying flat, the streaming blood pumping into the dry, greedy sand.

'Hell, Jim, he coughed. 'I – never figgered more – o' them.'

'Me neither,' Sudden told him grimly, 'Juano's bucks musta lost Quincy's trail an' doubled back to find it again. Them three was scouts: the others can't be far off.' He put an arm under Tucson's shoulder and raised him. 'I got to get yu out o' here,' he said. Tucson groaned in agony, and his face went a pasty shade of grey.

'No use . . .' he panted. 'Somethin' – busted, inside.'

His eyes were narrowed against the burning pain of his wound, and the veins in his temple throbbed visibly. His face was quite white now, tinged with the colour of the sunrise. Already, above the distant hills, a ball of flame heralded by a blaze of red gold, was pushing up into the sky. As yet the valleys and gulches surrounding them were deep in shadow, and any one of them could hide a thousand Apaches.

'Them bucks musta had hosses,' Sudden told his comrade. 'Yu rest easy a moment, Tucson; I'll take a look-see.'

He found the three ponies tethered to a bush not fifty yards away, and tied to the saddles were two water canteens with the legend 'U.S.' stencilled on them.

'Army,' muttered Sudden, seeing in his mind's eye the ambush: the soldiers fighting back, the killings, the stripping of the soldier dead. 'Water's water,' he said resolutely. 'No matter what it comes in.' He also found two rifles, some ammunition pouches, also stencilled with Army markings, and a short Apache bow with a quiver of arrows. All of these he loaded on to one horse, and led it, with another, back to where he had left Tucson. At the sound of his approach, Tucson opened his eyes.

'Hosses!' he gasped. 'Jim, if – yu ain't . . .' He shook his head. 'Shore – a pity – I can't git aboard – one.'

'Take some water,' Sudden told him, offering a canteen. The giant swigged greedily, his Adam's apple bobbing, until the Texan snatched the canteen away.

'Too much is as bad as not enough, Tucson,' he told his companion. 'Yu feel any better?'

'A mite, Jim,' admitted Tucson. 'A mite.'

'Then yu'd better try gettin' on board one o' these ponies, or we're goners shore,' Sudden said grimly.

The frown of puzzlement on Tucson's face was wiped off when Sudden explained this curt command. 'The rest o' them just turned up,' he said, pointing with his chin. Turning his head, Tucson could see them outlined against the rim of a ridge perhaps half a mile away to the west, well-spaced out, the lance points catching the sunlight, and the mottled colours of their warpaint sharp and clear in the morning light.

Sudden squinted at the band. Seven, eight, nine of them. It couldn't be Juano, then. So, it must be Manolito! The Apaches must have split up to cover both escape routes. Juano had taken the desert route and Manolito the valley. Finding no trace of the fugitives, he had cut across to join forces with the rest of the war party, and his scouts finding Sudden's tiny fire, had led him to them. A curse escaped Sudden's tightly pressed lips. They were in no condition to fight, and Tucson wouldn't be able to hold on long even if he got him mounted. He opened the breech of one of the rifles and loaded it.

'Help me – up.'

Tucson's voice was hard, and there was a returned strength in it which surprised the Texan. Tucson had rolled on to his side, and though his eyes swam with pain, he was trying to rise. Putting an arm under Tucson's, the puncher helped the giant up. Painfully, his full weight on Sudden, Tucson got to his feet.

'Help – put me on – that pony,' was Tucson's next command, and he lurched over towards the pinto, which skittered slightly at the smell of Tucson's blood.

'Get up on his right-side,' Tucson said. ''Paches don't – mount—'

'—I know, I know,' Sudden told him. 'Take it steady, Tucson.'

The big man was referring to the Indian custom of mounting their ponies from the right hand side. Any attempt to mount from the left, as was normal range practice, would result in the animals shying.

With a deep groan, Tucson slid on to the horse's back,

swaying, his head lolling. 'Tie – my feet, Jim,' he whispered. His chin came up defiantly, drawing upon his last reserves of strength.

A quick glance showed Sudden that the Apaches had seen them. With a shrill cry they put their horses to the gallop, sweeping down the long shallow side of the ridge, moving in a fast, deadly sweeping arc towards the two men. Sudden lashed the big man's feet beneath the pony's belly and at Tucson's command handed the giant one of the rifles and a handful of cartridges.

'That's – dandy,' Tucson gritted. 'Jim – lissen to me. I ain't got – long. Yu make – yore run, yu hear?'

'No! Yo're ridin' with me!' Sudden told him flatly.

Tucson cocked the rifle in his hands and pointed it at Sudden, gritting his teeth against the slight motion of the pinto.

'Do like I – tell yu,' he said, grimacing with pain. 'There's no point in – both of us gettin' kilt. Yu – find that gal. Tell her – tell her what I – done.' He managed a smile. 'Shore sorry – we never finished – that fight. Yu – scrap real – good.'

Without another word, he wheeled the pony about and slashed it across the rump with the barrel of the rifle. With a snorted squeal of rage the pinto leaped into a gallop, thundering at top speed directly across the path of the advancing war-party. Tucson had regained his balance now, and with his feet tied, had both hands free to load and fire the rifle. Right across the front of the advance he rode, blasting a hail of bullets into the Apaches, toppling one, two, three warriors from their horses before the Apaches had recovered from their surprise. The last thing that they had expected was to be attacked, and with a screech of hatred they fell back, their line breaking. Then they regrouped to thunder in pursuit of the speeding Tucson, who was half turned in the saddle, pulling the horse around in a quarter turn to pour more shots into the milling Indians.

Sudden heard the thin defiant yell the giant gave as another Indian slid out of his saddle, and then the Apaches started firing, the shots flat and dead, sounding like the snapping of twigs. Tucson's horse dropped out of sight behind the level of a ridge perhaps a mile away, the Apaches in hot pursuit. Now Sudden swung into the saddle of the Apache pony, booting it into a dead run, away from the scene of one of the bravest actions he had ever witnessed. Far off, now, he could hear the sound of the guns, and then he could hear nothing except the thunder of his pony's hoofs. Tucson's ride was over.

CHAPTER FOURTEEN

THEY had ridden long miles over mighty stretches of bare desert, crossed flat topped mesas, toiled up wide sweeping slopes of shifting sand, and threaded their way through tracts where Nature, by some internal convulsion, had disrupted the land into little hills, rocky gulches, and ravines. Above them a sun of polished brass poured down its blinding rays. A desolate and sterile land, without water or timber, its scant vegetation consisting of sage, greasewood, mesquite and cactus. Well might men shudder at the prospect of crossing such a trackless waste. The sand reflected the sun's rays back into their faces, and they seemed at times to be wading through a lake of shimmering heat.

'Well, one thing,' Quincy said, his voice rusty with thirst. 'No preacher'll be able to scare me with hellfire no more. Gawd! To think o' the times I coulda gone swimmin' an' didn't.'

He turned his dust-reddened eyes upon the flaming disc in the heavens and mouthed a curse beneath the handkerchief which covered the lower part of his face.

'How far yu reckon we got to go?' croaked Shiloh. To emphasize his question he held up the water canteen and shook it. The thin swish of liquid indicated a perilously low level, and Quincy frowned. 'Just about make 'er, I'd reckon,' he grunted. 'Providin' we don't get no more trouble from them warwhoops.'

There had been no sign of Apaches for the past twenty four hours, but neither of the scalphunters was foolish enough to believe that this automatically meant they had outdistanced the Indians. 'It's when yu don't see the red sons that yu got to most ready for 'em,' was Shiloh's unspoken thought. He glanced at the girl, riding slumped in her saddle, and then at Rusty, who favoured him with a look of pure detestation. Shiloh scowled. 'Yu got yore come-uppance to get, sonny,' he muttered. 'An' yo're a-goin' to get it shore.'

He squinted off to the left, lining up their route mentally with his own picture of the land through which they were passing. They had swung west, away from the route that Sudden had planned, the one which would have led almost due south to Fort Cochise. That route would have brought them out of the desert within a day, but Shiloh's plan necessitated one further day in the desert. By evening, he figured, they would reach the edge of the desert, and then, skirting it, move down the long valley which dropped through the badlands to Wilderness.

He signalled with his eyes, and Quincy edged his horse alongside.

'What's up?' he asked.

'By my reckonin' we oughta be out o' this hellhole in a coupla hours,' Shiloh replied. 'We got to see if the kid's goin' to do like he's told.'

'Yu reckon he will? He was killin' mad when we left Sudden for the Injuns.'

'We got a double hold on him,' Shiloh leered. 'Fust off, he's sweet on the gal. Second, he still thinks he beefed that cardsharp in Bisbee. He ain't goin' to give us no trouble. He knows the gal'll get back to her ol' man on'y if the reward's delivered. And if the kid makes him understand that she won't lack for some lovin' I'm guessin' Davis'll come across pretty pronto.'

Even as he uttered the infamous suggestion, Shiloh's lustful eyes devoured the girl, and his thin lips uncovered his stained teeth in a bestial grimace. Quincy felt a shudder of repugnance. Hardened brute though he was, there were times when Shiloh Platt turned his stomach. The half-breed was a mean one, a man who enjoyed spilling blood.

'Don't yu reckon we better just make shore afore we turn him loose?' he suggested. 'He's crazy enough to try somethin' stupid.'

'Don't yu worry none,' leered Shiloh. 'I won't be takin' no chances on him. He's what yu might call – dispensable.' He spurred forward until he caught Rusty's eye, then signalled him aside.

'What yu want, Shiloh?' he asked shortly. 'Spit 'er out; I'd as lief ride alongside a polecat.'

Shiloh's breath hissed between his teeth but he controlled his passion. 'We're goin' to be clear o' the desert afore long, Rusty,' he began ingratiatingly. 'Time yu learned what part yo're goin' to play.'

'I'll have nothin' to do with yore dirty plans!' snapped Rusty angrily. Quincy raised his eyebrows quizzically.

'Don't yu want the gal to get home safe, sonny?'

'Yu know damned well I do,' replied Rusty. 'But I ain't shore that's what yu two skunks is plannin'.'

'Why, o' course it is, o' course it is,' Shiloh said smoothly. 'All we want is the reward, kid. Yu don't deny we've earned it?'

'By God!' Rusty swore. 'Ah, what's the use? Yu don't know the difference anyway. I'm tellin' yu just one thing: if playin' any part in yore dirty schemes is a condition o' gettin' Barbara home safe, I ain't buyin'!'

'I think yu'd better,' Shiloh warned him, a deadly thinness in his voice. 'She could get – hurt.'

'If'n yu don't do what yo're told,' added Quincy.

Rusty's face went white with anger. 'Yu so much as lay a finger on her, and I'll hunt yu to the ends of the earth an' kill yu like the mongrel yu are!' he gritted.

Platt let his anger come to the surface for a moment, and he gestured at Rusty's gunbelt, looped around his saddlehorn, hissing: 'What yu aimin' to do, kid? Beat out my brains with a rock?'

'What is it yu want me to do?' the boy asked, as defiance fled his expression and his shoulders slumped.

'That's more like it, sonny,' Quincy said encouragingly. 'I allus figgered yu was a sensible kid.'

'Get to it,' ground out the boy.

'She's simple enough,' Shiloh told him. 'Yu ride in to Tucson an' roust up ol' man Davis. Yu tell him we got his daughter, an' the price to him is twenty thousand dollars.'

'Yo're mad!' Rusty gasped. 'He'll never pay it!'

'He better,' was the meaningful reply. 'I'd hate to think o' the consequences if he don't.' His evil eyes touched the girl and rage seared through Rusty at what he saw in them. Then once more his shoulders dropped, as though he had realized once more the impossibility of fighting.

'I guess there ain't much choice at that,' he managed.

'The gal'll give yu somethin' o' hers to identify yoreself, an' she can write a note. Davis has to come along – no sheriff, no posse – yu tell him. Any double-cross an' it's the gal who'll suffer. Yu make shore he knows that.'

Rusty nodded. 'I'll need a gun,' he said.

Shiloh looked up, as though the thought had not previously occurred to him. 'Course yu will,' he replied. 'Can't take no chances on them warwhoops stoppin' yu gettin' to Tucson.' He turned aside, and drew the youngster's gun from its holster.

'Here y'are, kid,' he called, and tossed the gun underhand to the youngster, who caught it neatly and – without checking it – thrust it into the waist band of his pants. Platt smirked; it could not have worked better had he been able to control it.

'I'll jest scribble them instructions,' he said, pulling a notebook from his saddlebag, and moistening a stub of pencil on the tip of his tongue. He motioned Quincy not to move as the scarfaced man looked sharply up: Rusty was edging his horse sideways gradually, placing himself in a position directly between Barbara Davis and the two scalphunters. Shiloh looked up in assumed astonishment as Rusty rapped out a command: 'Shiloh! Quincy! Unbuckle yore gun belts an' let 'em drop!'

The gun pointed rock-steady at the mid-point between Shiloh and Quincy, who sat unmoving. A grin of evil glee was twitching at the corners of the half-breed's mouth.

'Yu heard me!' Rusty said, impatience thinning his tone. 'I'm countin' three: if yu ain't shucked yore gunbelts by then, I'm goin' to shoot 'em off yu!' Over his shoulder he added 'Barbara! When I give the word, yu ride like H-ades for the south, yu hear?'

Barbara nodded tensely; would Rusty's desperate gamble pay off? Almost as if in answer to her thought, Shiloh's face twisted into a vicious sneer.

'Fire away, yu dolt!' he hissed. 'Did yu think I'd be fool enough to give yu a loaded gun without first testin' yore loyalty?'

The knowledge that he had been duped flooded Rusty's eyes, and the empty click as he pulled the trigger of the six-gun confirmed it: the half-breed had been one step ahead of him the entire way. Rusty had played along with Shiloh in the hope of getting his hands upon a weapon; Shiloh had out-thought and outwitted him. With a shout of pure anger, he rammed the spurs into his horse's flanks, and the animal lunged forward at Shiloh. In the same moment, Rusty hurled the heavy sixgun at Quincy's head. The weapon smashed into Quincy's forehead and he swayed backwards, almost falling from the saddle, his senses reeling.

Even as Rusty hurtled towards him, however, the half-breed's hand darted for the gun at his side. 'Ah, would yu?' he snarled, and flame lanced from the weapon. Rusty slewed sideways out of the saddle, hitting the earth and lying limp; he kicked once, and blood matted his hair. A thin keening scream broke from Barbara Davis's lips, and went on until

Shiloh stalked across to where she stood and slapped her rudely across the face. The girl went silent with a shocked gasp.

Quincy was dabbing his forehead with a kerchief; the gun had raised a lump on his forehead just below the hairline and blood trickled from it. Shiloh regarded the fallen Rusty dispassionately.

'Better to find out now that he'd double-cross us,' he grated. 'When it comes to gettin' that money, we don't want no slip-ups.'

'Is he dead?' the scarfaced one wanted to know.

'I don't know,' Shiloh said callously, 'an' what's more I ain't carin'. He played his hand, an' he lost.'

'The question is – what do we do now?' Quincy asked. Shiloh shrugged and was about to speak when a movement on a far hillside caught his eye. He froze for a moment, and then pointed with a finger which trembled slightly.

'There's yore answer,' he said. 'We better ride!'

Following the half-breed's pointing gesture, Quincy saw riders sweeping down the long slope of a ridge in the near distance. The Apaches were coming.

'Git on yore hoss!' he snapped to the girl, who was bending beside the prone body of Rusty, dabbing the blood away with a strip of cloth. He dragged her away from the body, and Barbara screamed at him, arching her lithe young body, trying to rake Quincy's eyes with her fingernails. 'He's alive!' she sobbed. 'He's alive, he's alive! Oh, for pity's sake don't leave him there to die!'

'What yu want me to do, carry him?' Ignoring the girl's sobs, Quincy tossed her bodily on to the back of her horse, and slashed it across the rump, sending it galloping off as he swung into his own saddle, catching up with the girl and Shiloh, heading in a last long rocketing run for the edge of the desert and the lawless town in Wilderness Canyon.

CHAPTER FIFTEEN

Through the bright desert day Sudden had pushed the wiry little Apache pony hard. The clear, invigorating morning air had revived his aching body, aided by the magnificent constitution born of long days in the open, simple food, and the casual health of a big cat. Now the blistering heat of afternoon had slacked his progress, and Sudden moved more slowly. Yet inexorably he pushed on, and the miles dropped beneath the feet of the horse.

'If Apaches can run in this heat, damn' if I can't ride in it,' he gritted, as he pushed on through long stretches of empty desert, sometimes stopping to check the traces he was following. Juano's warriors had made no effort to conceal their passing; they had no reason to suppose that anyone was following them, or to fear anyone who was. He rode on through the deathly silence of the desert, frowning slightly in puzzlement at the south-westerly direction into which the trail was veering. That they were following Shiloh there was no doubt; but why had the half-breed deliberately elected to go deeper into the desert instead of running for the shelter of Fort Cochise? 'Even if he stayed clear o' the Fort itself – an' bein' as Quince was along, I'd reckon he would – he'd've still been inside the patrol area. Mister Shiloh Platt must have some other cards to slide from up his sleeve.' As the tracks continued south-west, Sudden reviewed in his mind the layout of the country surrounding him. Fort Cochise lay to the south-east now, and between it and the desert lay the ridges and folds of what was known as The Wilderness. They were badlands: gouged-out canyons, twisted rock formations, as bleak as the surface of the moon. The Wilderness was skirted on the south by the Fort Cochise road and on the west by the valley road leading to Apache Wells and on to Phoenix. Shiloh would not head straight for Tucson. Which left only one place he could possibly head for to find safety: Wilderness!

Sudden recalled the stories he had heard about the town. Bleke had mentioned it during their long talk in Tucson, but they had both agreed that the threat of an Indian war overshadowed the necessity of doing something about Wilderness. 'The town's a cesspool, Jim,' Bleke had barked. 'One o' these days it's goin' to need cleanin' out.'

The little pony willingly responded to Sudden's urging and the man from Texas pushed on, his face grim. Around him, he sensed the fertile, unseen life of the desert. Insects, spiders, birds, lizards, snakes, rats, rabbits – all flourished unseen in the thickets of cactus and cholla. Once, he saw a zebra-tailed lizard scurry across the rocks, its forelegs dangling against its chest; on a flat stretch of hot sand a horned toad regarded him with a flatulent eye, not deigning to move aside at the thunder of hoofs.

Sudden eased the pony up a hogback ridge, careful to keep his silhouette below the skyline. Dismounting, he tied the Apache rope hackamore to a stunted bush which clung to the bare slope and eased himself forward on his belly, using elbows and knees for leverage, rifle cradled across his arms. If his calculations were correct, he was close behind Juano and his braves. If he over-ran them, his own efforts and the brave sacrifice of Tucson would have been for nothing: he would be ruthlessly dealt with by the Apaches.

'An' one try a week's all I aim to give 'em,' he muttered with a grin. He reached the crest of the ridge, and peered cautiously over. An explosive exclamation escaped his lips. 'My Gawd!' he breathed.

Below him, in almost a straight line from where he lay on the hot rimrock, Juano and his warriors stood in a circle around a squat saguaro cactus. Lashed to its spiky stem, the cruel barbs biting deeply into his body, Sudden made out the slumped form of Rusty. The boy's face was twisted with pain, and his hair was matted with blood. His head was held back, rigid, away from something which Juano held before the youngster's face. Straining his keen gaze, Sudden made out the object in the Apache's grip: it was a male rattler! Juano's hand held the ugly reptile just behind its flat, diamond-patterned head, while his left hand and arm firmly clamped the threshing, writhing body so that the snake could not tear itself out of his grasp. The rattler's darting tongue flickered in and out, carrying the hated, feared smell of humans to the tiny brain, making the creature bare its venom-carrying fangs in a terrible grimace. Juano thrust the snake within an inch of Rusty's face and the youngster shrank involuntarily back. In doing so he impaled his body harder upon the torturing barbs of the cactus, and despite himself, a cry of pain escaped his compressed lips, already bloody where he had bitten them.

'You tell!' Juano shouted at him. 'Why girl important?'

'Go – to – hell!' Rusty managed, twisting his head to keep the gaping reptile's head as far from his face as possible.

'Speak!' hissed Juano. He thrust the snake forward. Rusty flinched and again the wicked spikes of the saguaro sank deeeper into the unprotected flesh of his back. A thin scream of pain was wrung from his lips.

'You tell!' the Apache spat. 'They go Tucson? They go town-in-canyon? You tell!'

Rusty shook his head. 'They – they're headin' for Tucson.'

'You lie!' snarled Juano. 'Now Juano know. Going other town. Now you die!'

Again he thrust the snake forward, this time releasing its head; but in that same second a bullet smashed the ugly creature's striking face into a thousand pieces, a second blasted Juano off his feet, a neat hole between the mad eyes, a third and fourth dropped the warriors at either side of the Apache leader.

'Jim!' Rusty cried.

Sudden had worked his way down the side of the ridge while Juano and his braves were engrossed in torturing the boy. He stood now like a grim spectre of death at the head of the shallow gully which had concealed him long enough to sneak within ten yards of the bunched Apaches and now he mercilessly turned the deadly brilliance of his shooting upon them.

His fifth shot spun one of the warriors screaming to the ground, the sixth cartwheeling yet another off his feet. Now the Apaches reacted instantly to the shock of Sudden's appearance, falling flat or scattering to avoid the murderous accuracy of the Texan's shooting. One leaped into a dead run towards Sudden, a screeching yell of insane hatred shrieking from his throat. The Texan had dropped to one knee, making himself a smaller target, and again the Winchester barked, cutting the Apache down in mid-stride, whirling him aside like a dried leaf. Without hesitation, Sudden dashed forward, weaving as he ran towards the saguaro where Rusty watched helplessly. Apache bullets whispered around the lithe form of the running man; one tugged gently at his sleeve, and another burned across the upper muscle of his left arm and then he was beside Rusty. A sweeping slash of the knife in his hand freed the boy, who dived to the ground, rolling, to snatch up the rifle dropped by one of the fallen Apaches. Rusty came to his feet to meet the screeching rush of the last two Apaches, frantically working the bolt of the old-fashioned weapon. His bullet stopped one of them as if the Apache had run into a brick wall. The other moved in a crouching run towards Sudden, leaping at the Texan in a tigerish bound as Sudden reversed the empty Winchester smoothly, grasping the barrel with both hands. He whirled it in a short and vicious arc which ended as the butt caught the Indian in mid-leap. The mighty blow split the Apache's skull like a melon, making a dull sound like that of a butcher's axe hitting a side of beef. It dropped the Indian in a quivering, lifeless heap to the dusty ground. A sifting curtain of dust stirred slightly in the still air and then settled, as Sudden tossed the useless rifle aside and straightened up warily.

'Gawd alive!' breathed Rusty. 'Now wonder they call yu Sudden!'

'They don't,' the Texan told him. 'Not if they like me.'

Rusty was instantly contrite. 'Jim, I'm a fool,' he apologized. 'I just never seen anythin' like it in my life! Where in 'ell did yu spring from anyways? I figgered yu was cashed for shore.'

'So did he,' Sudden said, pointing to the still form of the dead Juano. 'If he hadn't 'a' been so wrapped up in teasin' yu with that rattler . . .'

Rusty shook his head. 'I know it,' he said quietly. 'Jim, I'm thankin' yu.'

'Shucks, no call to do that,' Sudden told him with a smile. 'Yu all right?'

'I been better,' Rusty admitted, 'but I'll do.'

In a few terse words, he described the events which had led up to his being shot by Shiloh; and how Juano had found him lying half-conscious in the open desert.

'He shore played in pore luck,' remarked Rusty with a glance at the dead Apache. 'I still can't figger out why he didn't just kill me an' ride on after Quincy an' Shiloh.'

'Some men is just born pizen mean,' Sudden said, and there was that in his voice which convinced Rusty that his friend was speaking from deep inside some bitter, personal memory. 'They don't have to be Apaches,' Sudden went on. 'They's plenty o' whites no better, mebbe wuss; men what just can't resist gloatin', torturin' a helpless prisoner. He was one. He did it once too often.'

Despite himself, Rusty felt a shiver run across his skin at Sudden's cold epitaph for the Apache. Many years later, when he heard for the first time of Sudden's finding of the two men he had sought so long, and of his final reckoning with them, Rusty would remember this moment.*

As if making an effort of will, Sudden looked around. 'Pick up all the guns an' take any ca'tridges yu find. If any o' these bucks got bows, break 'em. I'll check their hosses. We don't want to leave nothin' here for their sidekicks to use again.'

Rusty looked a question, and Sudden grinned. 'Yu figger it was all over, Rusty? Hell, no! There's another bunch o' them on my tail, an' they've got a much smarter *hombre* than Juano to lead 'em. I'd as lief not be here when they arrive an' find this.'

He lifted his chin to indicate the scattered corpses of the slain Apaches. Rusty nodded his agreement. If they had been prized prey for their pursuers before, now they would be hunted with the special zeal the Apaches reserved for their bitterest enemies. Walking stiffly, favouring his thorn-slashed muscles, Rusty did as he was bid. They bundled all the rifles into a saddle blanket and mounted the ponies which Sudden led up from their place of concealment in the wash below.

'We played in fool's luck,' Sudden announced. He held up his own guns, which he had found looped upon what must have been Juano's mustang, and handed a second belt to Rusty, who strapped it on with a grim smile.

'Now!' he vowed, his face set. 'Now, Mister Shiloh Platt. This time I got a gun what's loaded!'

Sudden turned his pony's head to the south-west.

'Yu know,' he said thoughtfully. 'I ain't shore I didn't

* **Related in THE RANGE ROBBERS (Corgi Books)**

waste a shot back there.' Rusty frowned at him. 'I don't get yu, Jim,' he said.

Sudden grinned. 'I salivated that pore ol' rattler, didn't I?'

Rusty nodded, still mystified. 'Which I'm thankin' yu,' he said. 'Yu reckon that was a wasted shot, yu oughta bin standin' where I was.'

Sudden shook his head. 'Naw,' he scoffed. 'From the look on yore face a minnit ago, I'd say if that ol' daddy rattler'd bit yu, he'd a got a wuss pizenin' than he give!' A broad grin spread across his face as Rusty replied to this slander in terms neither polite nor printable. 'That's better,' Sudden said, and again there was a hint of sadness in his voice. 'Lookin' for revenge sometimes makes a feller blind to everythin' else.'

He kicked the pony into a gallop and led the way down the gully towards the south-west, towards the edge of the desert and the jumble of badlands which the Apaches had named Place-where-nothing-lives: the Wilderness!

CHAPTER SIXTEEN

'ANYTHING GOES IN WILDERNESS!'

THE crude sign stood by the roadside – not much more than a track – which petered out on the northern side of the straggling collection of buildings which was Wilderness. It was not a big town, and its inhabitants were not particularly proud of it; as a consequence, Wilderness fell some way short of being a beauty spot. Its roughly-defined street, sloping slightly up the canyon in which the town stood, was hock-deep in the gypsum-like desert dust, rutted with hoofmarks and wagon tracks. The clutter of habitations bordering the street were for the most part of rough adobe, squat unlovely blocks with tiny windows, their only purpose to provide shelter from the merciless sun. There were a few buildings of slightly larger dimensions; one of these was the saloon, another a stable. Between the buildings, the litter of years had accumulated in careless piles inhabited by rats and a few starving cats which hunted them. At the southern end of the canyon a rickety footbridge spanned a deep gully which in the brief rainy season became a foam-flecked torrent.

Upon the street moved every frontier type: the eye caught here a glimpse of the soft tones of fringed and beaded buckskins, there the flashing colours of a Mexican *serape*. Roughly-dressed rowdies; dark-suited, prosperous-looking men; gaudily-brilliant vaqueroes waiting for things to cool off in California or old Mexico; all mingled freely on the crowded street. Every man walked heavily armed, for there was only one law in Wilderness: gun law. Judge Colt arbitrated in all disputes, and there was no appeal against his decisions.

Quincy gazed down upon the bustling street from the window of a cabin high on a slope at the northern edge of the town.

'Shore is a purty layout, Shiloh,' he observed. 'Ain't nobody likely to get within a hundred yards o' this place without we see 'em.'

'I know it,' Shiloh said, a satisfied smirk on his face.

The cabin was gloomy and covered with a film of dust inside and out. It stood on a shelving slope which backed up to a high ridge on the lower part of the canyon wall. A few rough chairs, a table with a candle stuck in its own grease upon it, a crude bunk in the corner – these were all the furnishings. There was only one window, and it commanded the open space before the cabin, looking out upon the poor huddle of Wilderness.

'We got to get some grub, an' mebbe somethin' to drink,' Shiloh said, as if thinking out loud. 'Ain't no tellin' how long we'll be here.'

His eyes touched Barbara Davis, who had slumped down upon the unkempt bunk, listless and weary after the long ride across the badlands. It seemed to the girl as if her every hope had been dashed by her murderous captors, and that there was no chance of escaping their ruthless clutches. Deep in the eyes of Shiloh Platt she had detected a light which stirred the deepest and most primitive fears in her breast, making her more afraid than she had ever been in her life. Her mind returned constantly to the thought of Rusty, left lying wounded, perhaps dying, in the path of the oncoming Apaches. The thought of the young man she had grown to respect and admire falling into those vengeful hands made the girl shudder, and tears filmed her eyes as she recalled his thoughtful kindnesses.

Quincy buckled on his gunbelt, and opened the door.

'I'll get some supplies,' he offered. 'Find out what the word is in town. I'll take my time,' he added with an evil leer at Shiloh. 'Don't yu do nothin' I wouldn't do.' Shiloh nodded, and waited until the door banged shut before he turned to the girl, who shrank backward from his burning gaze.

'I reckon yore Daddy's goin' to be some surprised to hear from yu,' he ventured. 'He probably figgers yo're long since dead.'

'There have been times – just lately – when I wished that were true,' Barbara told him.

'Aw don't say that, girl!' Shiloh's voice was thick and husky. 'Yu an' me – we're goin' to get to know each other real good. We're goin' to have plenty o' good times.'

Barbara Davis shuddered and did not answer, and a pin-point of anger kindled in the half-breed's eyes.

'Yu better learn to like me,' he scowled. 'Afore yu leave here, yu may be glad to do my biddin'.'

'Never!' the girl said bravely, and the anger gathered in the dark visage. 'Never's a mighty long time, my dear,' Shiloh said silkily, stretching out a clawlike hand to touch her shoulder. Barbara Davis got to her feet and walked to the other side of the room, her eyes wide with fear. Shiloh laughed, a harsh and unsympathetic sound; he enjoyed watching the terror building in her eyes. It made him feel strong, all-powerful. He had been scorned many times by women such as this one, who had seen in his dark face the evidence of the mongrel blood and contemptuously turned away. To possess such a one would therefore be all the more enjoyable. He licked his thin lips.

'Sit down, girl, sit down,' he said. 'I ain't goin' to hurt yu.' His smile was slow and wicked and Barbara felt a shiver touch her spine. She lifted her chin, trying not to let the fear show.

'I prefer to stand,' she said. 'I can keep further away from you.'

'As yu like,' he nodded. 'There's plenty o' time, plenty.

In the end yu'll come beggin' for a kind word. Beggin'.' He savoured the sound of the verb, his eyes gleaming. 'But – if yu want to make a game of it, that's all right with me.'

'Oh, why don't you let me go?' she burst out. 'I'll tell my father to pay you your reward. The two of you can take your money and go your way – won't you at least listen to me?'

Shiloh placed his hands behind his head and leaned back in the rickety chair. 'The two of us?' he repeated. 'Yu think I aim to share with that half-cracked madman? Yu must be outa yore head – the minnit he comes in through that door I'm goin' to blow his light out. Lions don't share with jackals!' The smile on his face was cold and devilish, his expression that of a fiend incarnate. It was then that Barbara Davis gave up hope.

* * *

John Davis strode aggressively into the patio of the house he had rented in Tucson. In it stood a white-haired old man who had every outward appearance of having crossed great distances at top speed. His clothes were sweat-streaked and dust-stained, and there was a heavy stubble on his grizzled chin. The man's eyes were bloodshot from lack of sleep and he swayed slightly with fatigue. He made no apology for his appearance, however, but asked simply: 'Yu John Davis?' Receiving a nod in affirmation he went on, 'I killed a pony gettin' here. I got news o' yore gal.'

'Barbara!' exclaimed Davis. He grabbed the old-timer's buckskin shirt. 'What do yu know of her? Where is she? Have yu seen her?'

Disengaging himself firmly from Davis's excited grip, the old man said: 'Take it easy, mister, an' listen good. My name's Eady. Tobias Eady. Yes, I seen yore daughter. A feller named Green brung her out of Apacheria an' managed to get to Apache Wells with her.'

'Is that where she is – Apache Wells?' demanded Davis.

'Wait, wait,' Eady said. 'Yu ain't heard it all. Jest relax a mite while I tell yu the whole story.'

Davis nodded impatiently. 'Get on with it, man,' he snapped.

'Yu shore ain't bustin' with gratitude,' observed Eady. 'I figger yo're entitled, however, or I'd take offence, some. Well, like I was sayin'. Green got to Apache Wells, on'y four other jaspers had latched on to him an' the gal. Mean *hombres* – scalphunters. We was hit by Apaches at the Wells; got out by a dodge Green thought up. He planned to make a run for Fort Cochise acrost the desert. I cut loose, figgerin' he might get whipsawed and these other jaspers take the gal. If that happened, yo're gal's in as bad danger as ever she was among the Cherry-cows, an' that's sartin.'

'Hell's teeth!' swore Davis. 'Yu think this Green feller had any chance o' reachin' Fort Cochise?'

'Nary much,' Eady replied. 'Easy enough findin' out. Yu could telegraph the Fort. If they ain't arrove, Green's been – disposed of, an' them scalphunters has got yore gal.'

'That's easy done,' Davis said, glad to take some positive action. He called out, and a young Mexican came running. 'Pedro,' Davis said, scribbling a note. 'Take this to the telegraph office. Get it sent right away. Wait for a reply.' He thrust the slip of paper into the boy's hand, then as the Mexican turned, added, 'Send Cliff Parker in here.' He explained this last command to Eady. 'Cliff's my new foreman. Apaches killed off some o' my crew when they burned my ranch, but most o' the boys was in Phoenix. I got fifteen men, an' I can raise ten more for every man on my payroll. If my gal ain't at Cochise, I'm goin' to give 'em guns an' go lookin' for them four jaspers. Yu got any idee where they might head for?'

'On'y one likely spot, I figger,' Eady remarked. Davis looked up sharply, and then nodded. 'O' course,' he said softly. 'Wilderness! Well, Eady, will yu ride with me? Yu know these buzzards by sight – I don't. If my gal's in that pesthole I'm goin' to ride in there an' scour it out. I'll burn every damn shack to the ground – and Gawd help any man who's laid a finger on my daughter!'

* * *

Quincy eased his pinto down the sloping street of Wilderness and pulled the animal to a stop outside the large edifice which housed the saloon which its owner, a one-time banker who had fled his native city after embezzling his depositors, had wryly named 'The Voice'. The subtlety of his choice of names was, however, lost upon his rough clientele. Jack Gardner did not mind; he was an observer of humanity, an educated man with a cynical humour made bold by the fact that he was dying of consumption. Like a more famous sufferer, the infamous Doc Holliday, Gardner was therefore unafraid of dying, at times even seemed to seek it by goading his dangerous customers; few cared to brave the whip of his vitriolic tongue.

The saloon was much the same as its counterparts throughout the West. Down one side stretched a long plank bar, behind which rose shelves stacked with bottles and glasses. In front of the bar was a sanded and sawdusted clear space, and tables and chairs filled that part of it at the end farthest from the batwing doors. Three kerosene lamps shone down upon perhaps two dozen men, some lined up at the bar, others desultorily playing cards at the tables, Squinting through the haze of blue tobacco smoke, Quincy studied the crowd. Apart from a few covert glances, no one took any notice of him. Curiosity was not a commodity encouraged in Wilderness; strangers were certainly no novelty anyway. Seeing no one he knew, Quincy pushed forward to the crowded bar and snapped his fingers.

'Have you lost a dog?' queried Gardner from the other

end of the bar. 'It hasn't been in here.' Several men guffawed, and Quincy's face darkened.

'I don't like yore sense o' humour overmuch,' he growled at Gardner, whose cold, thin face betrayed no fear at the words.

'An ill-favoured thing, sir, but mine own,' he quoted. 'You want a drink or did you come in here solely for the purpose of trading insults?'

'Gimme a drink,' snarled Quincy. 'Whisky!'

'Whisky it is, Mister—?'

'Quincy's the name. An' watch yore lip. I ain't fond o' smart jaspers what talk a lot.'

'You must be the life and soul of all the parties you're invited to,' observed Gardner unabashed. 'Excuse me, I see a gentleman.'

With this parting insult, which took a moment to register, he moved down the bar. His words sank slowly into Quincy's brain, and then the blood mounted to the scarred face.

'By the Almighty!' swore Quincy. 'If it warn't for—' He subsided. There was no point in starting a ruckus. This lawless town was their safe refuge; it would not do to jeopardize it so early in the game. When the ransom was paid, however . . his fingers tightened into a fist. Swallowing his anger, Quincy called the saloon-keeper over. 'I'm – beggin' yore pardon,' he mumbled. 'Been on the trail. A mite grouchy – we had Apaches tailin' us a lot o' the way.'

Gardner nodded. 'Glad you're not planning to shoot me,' he remarked. 'It does so lower the tone of the place. What can I do for you?'

'I need a couple o' bottles o' liquor,' Quincy told him, tossing a silver coin on to the bar in payment. 'An' mebbe yu can tell me whar I can buy some grub?'

Gardner was about to reply to the question when a cold voice cut across his words.

'Havin' a party, Quince?'

Quincy's jaw dropped as the question cut across the murmur of conversation. His arms filled with the four bottles he had just picked up, he swung around in amazement. There, standing near the doorway, idly leaning against a post, was Sudden. A cigarette drooped from his lips, the smoke spiralling thinly up past the slitted, icy eyes. Quincy's startled gaze scuttled about. Was he alone? How had he escaped, how got here? Those watching regarded the tableau in some surprise. There was something going on here which they did not understand. The big scarfaced man was as white as if he had seen a ghost; the question that the sardonic-looking stranger near the door had asked had badly jarred the bearded man.

As if divining their thoughts, Sudden repeated his question. Wilderness was an outlaw town, and its inhabitants knew that tone of voice well. Making as little noise or abrupt movement as was humanly possible, the onlookers began to imperceptibly shift their positions from any likely line of fire. A moment, two, and Quincy faced the slit-eyed Texan along an empty corridor lined by men who watched the confrontation with bated breath.

'What's the matter, Quincy?' Sudden's voice cut across the silence once again. 'Warn't yu expectin' to see me no more?'

'Damn yore eyes, Sudden – I thought yu was dead!' burst out the scalphunter. Every head in the room turned in unison at his words, and men craned to see the man who bore the name they had heard uttered. So this was Sudden! The lounging stance, the ice-cold steely eyes, the hands that never moved far from the tied-down sixguns – yes, he looked the part.

'I dunno what he's after that scarfaced jasper for,' one watcher muttered on the sidelines. 'But I'm purely happy it ain't me he wants.'

'Mebbe so,' another said. 'But that Quincy *hombre* shore ain't hornswoggled by 'im, Sudden or no.'

Indeed, Quincy's lips had curled. He did not know how Sudden had escaped the clutches of the Apaches; but it hardly mattered. What could he do, here in this lawless place? The fastest draw could not beat a bullet fired from ambush – and there were plenty who would do such a deed in this place. Sudden must know that if he revealed the girl's presence, there would be ten, twenty, half a hundred hard-bitten thieves only too ready to pit themselves against him for the five thousand dollars that returning the Davis girl would bring.

'Yo're bluffin', Sudden,' he scoffed. 'An' we both know it.'

'I ain't bluffin',' Sudden warned him. 'That'd be a bad mistake for yu to make. Yu know why I'm here. Where is Shiloh?'

'Go to hell!' Quincy snapped. 'I ain't talkin'.'

'Yu better,' came the cold reply. 'I ain't wasting time on a sidewinder like yu.'

Quincy shook his head doggedly. Without any warning, faster than the eye of any man in the saloon could follow, Sudden's hand swept downward, and a jet of flame spouted from his hip. The bullet burned across the top of Quincy's ear, flecking his cheek with blood.

'One inch to the right, an' yu'd be shakin' hands with Satan awready, Quincy,' Sudden told him grimly. 'Now – where's Shiloh?'

'Yo're so clever – find him yoreself!' sneered Quincy.

Again the sixgun barked. This time the bullet nicked off a piece of the scalphunter's earlobe, and warm blood trickled down his neck. A black rage welled inside the scarfaced man's heart, and those close to him saw a pulse begin to beat in a vein that swelled in Quincy's forehead. Had Shiloh Platt been there, he would have recognized those symptoms and quailed, knowing them for the onset of Quincy's uncontrolled madness. If Sudden also recognized these signs he gave no indication of it.

'Yo're runnin' out o' chances, Quincy,' the Texan said levelly. 'Where's Shiloh?'

An unearthly scream burst from Quincys lips, and foamy bubbles appeared at the corner of his mouth as he dropped the whisky bottles he had been cradling in his arms and with a filthy curse leaped straight for Sudden, his hand coming up from his belt clutching a long bladed knife which glinted with ugly highlights in the lamplight. Had his fell intent been realized, the knife would have been buried in Sudden's throat within another second, but Sudden was already moving He slashed sideways with the sixgun still in his hand, the heavy barrel smashing Quincy's wrist with a grinding crunch, sending the scalphunter reeling to the floor. The pain of the broken bones jarred the man into sanity, and he lay there huddled, whimpering.

'My Gawd,' whispered an onlooker. 'Will yu look at that Sudden jasper's face?'

Quincy looked; and what he saw in the Texan's eyes made him raise his good hand in an instinctive gesture of fear.

'I'll – talk,' he whined. 'Damn yu, I'll talk! Cabin – last one – on the north side o' the canyon.' He cradled his broken wrist to his body, rocking to and fro.

'Quincy,' Sudden told him. 'I'm servin' notice on yu. If I ever see that ugly mug o' yours again, I'm goin' to shoot it off. Get out o' town – get out o' this territory. If you ever cross my path again – I'll kill yu!'

There was a deadly levelness in his tone which carried more weight amongst these hardbitten onlookers than any shouted threat would have done.

'If I was that scarface feller, I'd be scratchin' dirt right now!' a burly fellow in a red shirt muttered to himself. Overhearing him, a man on his right added: 'Yu'd be eatin' my dust at that!'

It was at this moment that Rusty, whom Sudden had

sent to scout the other *cantinas* of the town, appeared in the frame of the batwings.

His searching gaze found his friend, took in the scene, the sprawled form of the whimpering Quincy.

'Jim,' he exclaimed. 'I heard shootin'. Was—'

'Was is right,' Sudden told him 'Come on – we got real work to do!'

He turned to join Rusty, and the younger man held the swinging door ready. It was as he did so that his face turned into a grimace of horror, for he had seen Quincy staggering to his feet behind the unsuspecting Sudden, the scarred face contorted with malevolence, and a sixgun lifting in the scalp-hunter's left hand.

Even as Rusty's mouth shaped to shout a warning, he saw Sudden turn in a smooth, fluent whirl, dropping to one knee as the hands moved with a speed defying sight. Before Quincy could even bring the gun in his hand level, Sudden's Colts boomed out, smashing the bearded man off his feet. Quincy bounced off the bar and fell in a crumpled heap into the jagged ruins of the shattered whisky bottles he had earlier dropped.

'Jee-hosophat!' someone whispered. 'Did yu see that?'

'Damned if I did,' admitted Jack Gardner at the bar. 'But I've never seen it better done.' He looked down at the bleeding body of Quincy and shook his head. 'What a waste – of good whisky.'

Gardner's unfeeling epitaph hung uncontradicted in the still air as the Texan and his young companion backed out of the saloon and, at a dead run, headed up the canyon towards the shack where Shiloh lay in hiding.

CHAPTER SEVENTEEN

'I'M lookin' for a jasper named Shiloh Platt!'

Caked with dust, his eyes glittering, the short thickset man burst through the batwing doors of Gardner's saloon and stood now belligerently upon its threshold, backed by a hard-eyed group of punchers with ported Winchesters. Jack Gardner moved along to the end of the bar.

'And who might you be?' he asked with raised eyebrows.

'I'm John Davis,' the rancher told him, and a sixgun appeared in the meaty paw. 'This is my visitin' card. Now – Shiloh Platt. Or a feller named Quincy. Where are they?'

Gardner nodded to the dead body. 'That's Quincy,' he said. 'You're the wrong side of early if you want to talk to him. I'd say you'll have to look sharp to talk to Shiloh Platt, as well. That Sudden fellow seemed in something of a hurry!'

'Sudden! exclaimed Eady, pushing forward. 'He's hyar?'

'Was here,' Gardner corrected the old-timer. 'He's gone looking for this Shiloh Platt.'

'Wharabouts?'

'A cabin somewhere to the north of town,' Gardner volunteered.

'We'll find it,' Davis nodded. He turned to face those watching him, and held up a hand for silence. 'I got a hundred an' fifty men with me,' he announced. 'They ain't lookin' for trouble no more'n I – but they ain't about to go out o' their way to dodge it none, neither. Reason I'm tellin' yu all this is simple – I'm servin' notice on this burg. In one hour from now I'm puttin' it to the torch!'

There was an uproar at this uncompromising announcement, and several of the denizens of the saloon pushed forward, their faces belligerent, ready for trouble. Behind

Davis, his top hand, Parker, levered the mechanism of his Winchester. The click-clack of the weapon stilled the strident voices like a switch; and Davis spoke again.

'If yu wanta argue the toss – my boys'll accommodate yu,' he told them levelly. 'I'm guessin' yu'd lose out. My advice is to grab what yu want to take with yu, an' get out o' town afore the deadline. One hour – then we come in, an' if we have to – we come in shootin'.'

'Lissen, Davis,' one tall man, standing at the front of the crowd interposed. 'Yu ain't the Law. Yu can't make us go.' Davis lifted the sixgun in his hand.

'Yo're wrong, mister,' he said. 'I got the Law right here with me.'

'Hell, Davis,' another called. 'We leave here, we're fair game for any lawman in the Territory.'

'I got Governor Bleke's word on this: there's a forty-eight hour amnesty on every man wanted by the Territory. Get out within that time an' yu won't be touched. If yo're still in Arizona after the amnesty runs out, then – hard luck. Now there ain't no more to say – I got other chores to do!' He hitched at his belt, and led his men out of the saloon, leaving behind him a crescendo of vociferous argument between those who had heard his words, and found in them a challenge to fight, and those who had heard in them a warning to run. In the end, one of them turned to Jack Gardner, who was calmly taking down bottles and glasses from his shelves, ignoring the uproar behind him completely.

'Jack – what in 'ell yu doin'?' the man asked.

'Why, Cassidy, I would have thought that even you could work that out,' the saloon-keeper replied silkily 'I'm packing up, moving on, shaking the dust of this place off my feet.'

'Hell, Jack, if yu go the town'll fold, an' yu know it!' another man shouted.

'Think what'll happen to the town if we stay,' Gardner said, a sly mischief in his eyes. 'Besides, "we only meet to part again", as the poet said.' He cast a swift glance about the saloon, and a derisive smile touched his thin lips. 'I never did like this place overmuch, anyway.'

* * *

There was about Shiloh Platt the instinctive caution of the scavenger. Like fox, coyote, or wolf, who lurk in wait to pounce upon their crippled prey, the half-breed had a kind of inborn intuition of threatening danger. He had heard the shots in 'The Voice' and stood now by the window, frowning. Had that insane dolt become embroiled in some sordid fracas in the town? Quincy had been a long time gone – maybe something was amiss. Shiloh rummaged in the saddlebags lying on the floor, and from them pulled a pair of powerful Army field-glasses, with which he scanned the rutted street of Wilderness. A curse escaped his tight-pressed lips as he descried Sudden and Rusty running up the street towards his hideout; and at the same time the party of riders led by John Davis boiling into the town across the footbridge at its southern end. The rancher was unknown to Shiloh; but the advent of a large band of armed men could only mean danger. It was typical of the man that he spent no time in wondering how his two most hated and feared adversaries had escaped the clutches of the Apaches, nor what had happened to his erstwhile partner. His mind rapidly evolved a desperate plan.

'Yo're pretty smart, Sudden!' he hissed. 'But I'll outsmart yu yet!'

Whirling about, he dragged Barbara Davis to her feet, and with ungentle and hastily expert skill lashed her wrists together in front of her with a rope, leaving perhaps six feet free. The end of this lead he looped around his own wrist and tied.

'Where I go, yu go!' he snarled. 'So yu better keep yore feet or that purty face is goin' to get scratched.'

'Where are we going?' asked Barbara, her bewilderment plain on her face. 'What is happening? Why are you running away?'

'Yore outlaw friend Sudden is headin' up here with that sneak kid yo're so fond of,' he scowled. 'I ain't aimin' to be here when he arrives!'

A bright gleam of hope kindled in Barbara's eyes only to be dashed by Shiloh's next words. Jerking cruelly on the rope to test it he sneered: 'Yu better hope they don't get too close, girlie, or I'll kill yu anyway!'

Without another word, he leaped to the window and emptied a sixgun down the slope at the advancing duo. Sudden and Rusty, caught in the open on the wide slope, had no choice but to drop flat and scuttle for the thin cover of a small pile of slatey rock. Without waiting further, Shiloh led Barbara out of the rear door of the cabin and on to the shale which skirted the foot of the ridge. A merciless tug on the rope nearly jerked her off-balance as she glanced over her shoulder. There seemed to be a lot of men coming up the slope, and she wondered who they could be; it was too far to clearly identify features. Then she gave her full concentration to the difficult task of keeping up with Shiloh as he climbed up and across the slope, heading for the jumbled rocks and cliffs which stood on the northern end of the canyon in which Wilderness lay.

Panting, sliding, cursing, dragging the girl after him, Shiloh Platt scrambled up the long, wide slope like some demented animal. He reached the crest with a gusty sigh of relief, pulling Barbara roughly after him, and shaking a defiant fist at the pursuers far below. His aim was simple; once in these uncharted badlands, he could lead whoever followed a fruitless chase, then double back to Wilderness, get horses, head somewhere else and once more present his demands for payment from Davis. 'It'll work, it'll work,' he convinced himself as he scrabbled along the crest of the ridge. 'An' if it don't – well, there's still the girl.' He feasted his eyes upon her for a moment, the thought giving him renewed strength. Barbara Davis collapsed, gasping for breath, as he halted.

'Come on, damn yu!' he cursed. 'Don't hang on me like that!'

'I'm – doing – my – best,' Barbara panted.

Shiloh led the way along the crest of a ridge leading to a deep, bowl-like depression in the mountainside. Some freak of nature had scooped from the rock a cup-shaped hollow perhaps a quarter of a mile across, littered with split rock and huge boulders. On its far side was a notch in the rim; this led into an arroyo which twisted off to the south and ran eventually into the gully which cut across the southern end of the street in Wilderness.

Dragging Barbara roughly along behind him, the half-breed headed for the rock bowl, and crossed its rim, sliding down the slope towards the bottom, the girl following helplessly. The slope levelled out, and as Shiloh staggered to his feet, the girl screamed. He whirled in annoyance, to see her pointing tensely at the crest on the side of the bowl farthest from them.

'Indians!' Barbara Davis shouted. 'Apaches!'

With a scream of frustrated rage, Shiloh whirled to turn back, but at that moment he saw the figure of Sudden appear at the top of the long slope he had just descended. Yanking out his gun, Shiloh threw two hasty shots at the pursuing Texan, who ducked back behind the lip of the hollow. Turning, Shiloh emptied his revolver at the Apaches, whisking one off his feet to slide limply downwards, bringing a small rock slide with him. Another screeched and fell, blood pumping from his thigh; and then they were out of sight in the flash of an eye, leaping for cover, diving out of range of Shiloh's reckless shots.

Thrusting fresh ammunition into the gun, Shiloh dragged

the girl into the floor of the hollow, heading erratically for a heaped pile of boulders where he could take cover. Thrusting the girl into the tiny space between the rocks, he whirled to face his enemies. Two Apaches had started to their feet on the rimrock, and he laughed wildly as his hasty shots chipped rocks from the ledge upon which they were standing, sending the Indians ducking for cover. There was a silence for a moment; and then Shiloh heard the racketing of sixgun fire from the direction in which he had just come. His lips curled in wolfish glee: so his pursuers had run into the Apaches!

'We'll let them entertain each other while we skedaddle,' he gloated to the girl. 'Come on, yu!'

Once more he dragged Barbara to her feet. He skittered across the floor of the bowl, moving quickly and carefully from rock pile to pile of boulders; no shots sought him, and a triumphant smile played around his cruel mouth. He would make it yet! Ahead of him, perhaps a hundred yards away, lay the break in the rimrock which led out of this depression and into the canyon. Between it and where he now crouched there was, however, no cover. He crouched behind the rocks, sweat matting his hair, his breath rasping in his throat. Barbara, her clothes dusty and tattered, leaned faintly against the rocks, struggling to catch her breath, half-swooning with exhaustion.

'On yore feet!' Shiloh snarled at her. 'Up, up!'

He jerked cruelly upon the rope, yanking the wilting girl to her feet by main force, and started out at a crouched run across the final flat stretch towards the cut in the rimrock. Barbara, reeling, was pulling on the rope, and the half-breed dragged on it impatiently. This unexpected pull spilled the girl off her feet, and she tumbled to the ground with a small cry, bringing Shiloh to a cursing stop.

'Get up, yu—!' he screamed

'I can't,' she panted pitifully, a trickle of blood coursing down her face from a cut she had suffered in falling. 'It's – my ankle. It's – I've hurt myself.'

Insane with rage and fear, Shiloh rained blows upon her, screaming at the girl to get up. He tugged mercilessly at the rope, tearing the tender skin of Barbara's wrists until she screamed with pain.

'It's – no – use,' she sobbed. 'I can't – I can't!'

Shiloh looked up to see an Apache loom startlingly in the rimrock gap. With a screech of triumph, the Indian leaped into a run, but before he had covered twenty feet, Shiloh had carefully aimed his sixgun and his bullet smashed the warrior to the ground.

Something buzzed past him and he turned in the opposite direction to see the figures of his white pursuers moving down the shaley slope on the far side of the bowl, and the puffs of smoke from their guns. Were they shooting at him? Or Apaches? It made no difference now. He had to get clear. A dozen Apaches slid over the rimrock equidistant with him and the gap in the bowl through which lay his only escape. He had the situation worked out now: the Apaches thought that the white men were trying to rescue him from them, and were intent on preventing any such rescue. 'They want me – or the gal,' he muttered, madness in his eyes. 'So – I'll just leave yu for them to play with, girlie. A pity, but – there's plenty o' wimmin.'

'You cowardly cur!' Barbara Davis breathed. 'Would you leave me to the Indians?'

Shiloh ground out an oath, and a sweeping blow from his half-clenched fist sent her reeling senseless to the rocky floor. With a bound, Shiloh regained his feet, and dashed for the gap in the rimrock, his sixgun blazing, driving the Apaches to cover. One of them yelled shrilly and pointed to the girl, and then Shiloh was through the gap and skittering down the far side of the rimrock lip, dropping in a sliding run to the floor of the arroyo sixty feet below – and safety.

CHAPTER EIGHTEEN

There was neither art now nor skill in the open fight between the white men and the Apaches. Ever since the attack on the ranch, Davis and his men had been itching for an opportunity to come to grips with their hated foes, and this, added to their superior numbers, was rapidly turning the tide of battle in their favour. In the forefront of the attack ran Sudden and Rusty, their guns blazing, pouring slugs into the scattered ranks of the screaming Apaches. Sudden drove a bullet into one painted face; a cowboy just to his left gasped and went down, blood pouring from a wound in his side. Racing across the floor of the depression, Sudden's second and third shots blasted a running warrior off his feet, and then the Texan was at Barbara Davis's side, with Rusty sliding in behind the boulders not ten seconds later. Together, they grabbed the swooning girl's arms and pulled her to cover, whirling to send a clutch of shots into two Apaches who had leaped after them, their axes raised, killing lust distorting the painted features. With a stifled curse, Sudden watched Shiloh leap over the rim of the depression and disappear. With a word to Rusty, he kicked off his boots.

'Keep me covered until I'm over that rimrock,' he shouted, 'I'm goin' after Shiloh!'

Before Rusty could protest, the Texan sped barefooted across the open ground, his twisting run making him impossible for the Apaches to hit. Rusty threw a scatter of shots towards the Apaches as they popped their heads out of cover to try a shot at the speeding Sudden; they ducked back, and then Sudden was out of sight beyond the rimrock. He slithered to a stop on the shaley slope, and assessed his position. Below, bearing off to the left, ran the arroyo. At its far end, where the canyon turned to the right again, he could see the stumbling figure of Shiloh, hardly more than a moving dot in the jumble of rock and desolation. To Sudden's right ran a ridge which ran in almost a straight line, raised like a furrow; and in a flash, the Texan realized that this ridge must finally come to an end at the same point as the arroyo down which Shiloh was presently heading.

'There's just a chance,' Sudden told himself. 'If I ain't forgot how to keep my balance!'

He stood, about to begin his perilous run, when a slithering sound made him whirl just in time to see an Apache launch himself in a flying leap through the opening in the rimrock. Half turned, Sudden drove three shots into the man's body, whisking the Apache backwards against the rock. For a moment, the Indian teetered there, then his eyes bulged in horror and he went lopsidedly off the rimrock and rolled downwards uncontrollably in a slithering welter of broken limbs.

'An' that's what'll happen to me if I slip,' the Texan muttered. Remembering that his gun was empty, his hand went instinctively to his cartridge belt. With a curse, he discovered that the loops were also empty: he was unarmed. There was no time to turn back, or Shiloh would be assured of freedom. Without a second thought, the Texan ran out on to the foot-wide rocky ridge, surefooted as any mountain goat, running as fast as he dared for the end of the ridge, which descended gradually as he traversed it, dropping to its eventual meeting with the floor of the arroyo.

The perspiration pouring from him, Sudden quartered down the last of the ridge and to the arroyo floor, finding a rocky ledge a little to his left which overhung the exit from the arroyo. He eased on to this and waited; within moments he heard the heaving gasps of Shiloh's breathing, and the half-breed came stumbling along the arroyo floor, dust-caked, bathed in sweat, but with a thin grin of triumph forming on his face as he saw the arroyo open out on to the plain.

In that moment, Sudden launched himself from the ledge, his arms wrapping around Shiloh, the sheer weight of his attack dragging the unsuspecting Shiloh to the ground with a bone-jarring thud.

With a scream of frustration and rage, Shiloh kicked and heaved clear, scrabbling away. Sudden leaped to his feet, reaching for the half-breed, ducking a murderous punch which, had it landed, might have ended the fight that instant. Shiloh came rushing in behind his punch, and Sudden chopped viciously at the man's head, knocking Shiloh to his knees in the soft sand. Shiloh's hand fumbled for the gun at his waist and Sudden, waiting, let him draw it from the holster before his well-aimed kick sent the weapon spinning from Shiloh's nerveless fingers. The half-breed came up without warning from his crouch, his clenched hand opening to hurl a handful of dust and grit straight into Sudden's eyes. Blinded, Sudden was defenceless as Shiloh slashed a wicked blow into his middle, folding Sudden forward, and then racked the Texan upright with a powerful uppercut. Sudden pawed the tears from his inflamed eyes, trying desperately to stay away from Shiloh's punches long enough to clear them and get some semblance of returned sight, while the scalphunter came mercilessly forward, throwing wicked blow after damaging punch into the Texan's unprotected body. Sudden fell forward into a clinch, grappling with Shiloh, trying to tie his arms up long enough to clear his eyes; the scalphunter brought up his knee in a wicked move which Sudden, sensing it coming, managed to take on the thigh. For a split second, Shiloh was off-balance, and in that moment, Sudden acted. He shot his arm upward rigidly, the heel of his right hand taking Shiloh beneath his snarling jaw, smashing his teeth together in a terrible impact which jarred the man back on to his heels, half-stunned. Merciless now himself, Sudden dashed the last of the grit from his eyes and prowled forward; for the first time Shiloh saw the cold ruthless light in the Texan's eyes, and as hope slipped away, desperation took its place. He threw wild and hurting punches at Sudden, punches which might have felled other men, but the Texan seemed impervious to them. He moved forward, relentless, unstoppable, and a final, mighty blow sent Shiloh full length, to lie on the flickering verges of consciousness in the dusty sand. Shiloh half-opened his eyes, turning his bruised face; the first thing he saw was his own pistol, lying half-buried in the soft sand. Waiting a second until his head was clear, he rolled over with a yell of triumph and grabbed it, sitting up and cocking the gun in one movement, his eyes slitted and evil, murder stalking through their deep darkness.

'So, Mister Sudden,' he whispered malevolently, 'Yu win, but yu lose!' Shiloh scrambled to his feet, facing Sudden, who was warily watching his every move. Shiloh cocked the revolver. 'I'm goin' to enjoy this,' he hissed. Then, as the pressure of his finger increased on the trigger, a movement behind the scalphunter caught Sudden's eye.

'Shiloh,' he whispered. 'Apaches! Behind yu!'

The half-breed laughed out loud. 'Sudden, yo're a pearl! Yu think I'm goin' to fall for that ol' chestn—'

Shhhwuck!

Shhhhwuck! Shhhhwuck!

For a brief moment, astonishment came into Shiloh's eyes as the arrows drove into his body. That faded, and into its place seeped a dying rage as Shiloh struggled to find enough strength to pull the trigger of the gun in his hand, to kill his Nemesis even as he himself died. But Shiloh's strength ran out along the arrow shafts with his blood, and he sank to the ground, his last word a curse. The feathered shafts quivered slightly and then all was still. Sudden did not move; he knew that he was helpless. Two warriors rose from hiding; again he was astonished at how near they had been without him seeing them. They were painted for war, and both had arrows fully drawn in their short bows, trained upon him.

'Howdy,' he said to them. His eyes flickered to Shiloh's gun; a good ten feet away, but there was a chance if he made a rolling dive . . .

'Do not think of that, Coyote!'

Sudden whirled as Manolito stepped out of the rocks behind his two warriors; his hand came up in the sign for peace.

Sudden returned the peace-sign gravely as Manolito regarded the Texan levelly from his position in the rocks.

'Scalphunter dead,' Manolito said. 'Other men go from town-in-canyon. Many warriors dead. It is enough.'

'Yu makin' peace-talk, Manolito?' Sudden asked.

'Maybe one day,' the Indian replied. 'Manolito owe you a life. Now it repaid. *Adios!*'

With a sort of salute, he wheeled and disappeared amongst the rocks. A few moments later, Sudden heard the ponies thundering away to the east. The Apaches were gone. Sudden found a flat-topped rock, and sat down on it, gazing in the direction the Apaches had taken.

'I guess if we work at it real hard for about the next six or seven hundred years,' he reflected, 'we'll mebbe begin to understand how an Injun's mind works.'

He was still sitting there, gazing into space, when Rusty and six of the Davis riders came riding down the arroyo and found him.

CHAPTER NINETEEN

'I DON'T care if he's an outlaw! I don't care if he's the biggest rogue as ever forked a saddle – I want Green to work for me, Bleke, an' yu got to make him do it!'

The speaker was John Davis. He stood once more in Governor Bleke's office, his chin thrust forward in that characteristic pose, glowering from beneath knitted brows.

Bleke smiled tolerantly. Many things had happened since the rancher had returned from Wilderness with Sudden and his daughter. Davis had left the town a smoking ruin, its motley inhabitants scattered. At Fort Cochise, Manolito had led his people in under a white flag and told the commanding officer that the Apache were no longer taking the war trail and wished to live in peace with their white brothers. The delighted Colonel Morris had telegraphed these glad tidings immediately to Bleke, who had been only too pleased to pass on such wonderful news to the people of Tucson. With the threat of war lifted, a holiday atmosphere prevailed in the little town.

Davis himself was shipping out supplies to rebuild his ranch-house, and smiling indulgently at the way that his daughter, now fully recovered from her ordeal in the mountains, stayed constantly within touching distance of the young man who had helped to rescue her. It had been but the work of an hour to discover that the gambler whom Rusty had thought he had killed was plying his trade, as healthy as a horse, in the same saloon in Bisbee. With that threat gone, Rusty had revealed his identity. His real name was Tom Freshwater, and his father owned a ranch over Los Alamos way. The news could hardly have pleased Davis more; his constant fear had always been that Barbara would end up married to some pasty-faced Tucson bank clerk see her so obviously in love with a cowman's son had d much to remove the deep lines of grief from Davis's fa With Sudden, however, he had been less fortunate. Despit all their pleading, he had shaken his head.

'I got a job to do,' he said doggedly to Davis, refusing all the man's offers. 'An' I got to do her.'

It was his departure which had prompted Davis to appeal finally to Governor Bleke, who had, after all, brought Green here in the first place. But Bleke was proving no help either.

'John,' the Governor reasoned. 'I don't own him. He's his own man – and like old Tobias Eady, he has his reasons for leaving.'

'Damn foolishness, if yu ask me!' snapped Davis. 'I offer him the job o' foreman on the new ranch – he turns me down. I tell him he's gotta take the reward for findin' Barbara – he tells me to give it to the kids as his weddin' present. Like to broke Rusty's heart when he wouldn't stay,' he mumbled.

Bleke spread his hands helplessly. 'John,' he said quietly. 'I want to remind you of something you said to me in this office not long ago. You said – and these were your exact words – you'd never met a man who couldn't be bought. Well, it's time you faced up to something: you've finally met one.'

'Well, hell an' blue blazes, Bleke!' exploded the rancher. 'All the more reason for wantin' him to stay an' help me to build the JD into a big ranch again.'

Bleke sighed and rose from his seat. He walked across the room and poured out two drinks from a decanter which stood on the table. One of these he held out to Davis, who took it.

'Maybe he'll come back one day, John,' he said softly to the rancher. 'When he's done – what he has to do.'

'By God, Bleke!' exclaimed Davis. 'I'll drink to that!'

* * *

A heavy rain had fallen the preceding night, and suddenly transformed the desert into a verdant garden. Leaves had burst from naked branches, and the bare ground was carpeted with tiny shoots and blades of green. Carpets of flowers – daisies, dandelions, verbenas – spread in a riot of colour across the bleak land, and upon the ugly cactus bright bursts of bloom softened the uncompromising outlines. Amid this loveliness, in a spot far out in the now-peaceful Apache land, a lone man stood bareheaded beside a fresh-dug grave upon which he had piled smooth desert stones. By the rough cross he had placed some wild flowers. He stood silently until his horse nickered softly behind him, and he allowed his breath to sigh out between his lips. 'Yo're right, ol' feller,' he told the horse. 'Time to be movin' on.'

Had there been anyone to see, they would have noted the gentleness in the grey-blue-eyes, the way that the hard lines upon the young face had softened as Sudden looked down for the last time upon the grave of the man who had saved his life.

He climbed into the saddle, and turned his horse's head towards the setting sun. A sad smile touched his lips. 'I'm thankin' yu, Tucson,' Sudden said softly. 'Yu – big dumb ox.'

THE END

SUDDEN by OLIVER STRANGE

A trio of land-grabbing brothers . . . a crooked town marshal . . . a beautiful woman . . . between them, they had the town under their heel. Now they meant to take the whole range, their weapons terror and destruction and murder.

Into this Arizona hell-town the Govenor sent Sudden. His instructions were brief: 'Clean it up', he said. 'No loose ends'. One man. A Texas outlaw with a badge. Sudden.

0 552 11797 8 - 95p